BEYOND THE CLOUDED WINDOW

A. A. Stevenson

DEDICATION

To my husband,

Your unwavering belief in me turned dreams into reality. Thank you for urging me to follow my heart, for seeing potential when I saw only doubts, and for walking beside me every step of the way. This story exists because of your love and encouragement.

TABLE OF CONTENT

CHAPTER 1

BEFORE

Izzy struggled to catch her breath as she stared at the two pink lines. No. No. No. Standing at the bathroom sink, anxious energy thrummed through her body. Unable to stand still, she began to pace the cold tiles beneath her bare feet. But the little white and pink stick lay on the ceramic, unmoved by her distress. She rechecked the instructions, praying she had made a mistake. Two lines. Positive test.

Disbelief gave way to a wave of dread and the implications of it all sliced through Izzy like a blade. She knew there was no going back. Trembling, she sank to her knees and pushed her shaking fingers through her hair. Her thoughts drifted to her stomach and the little blip of life growing there—known only to her. Awe flickered briefly, a firefly's glow in the dark. But it dimmed quickly under the weight of her reality—soon, she'd have to tell Liam. And Liam, with his notorious temper, was the last person she wanted to face with this news. *He's going to lose it.*

Izzy and Liam had met in their freshman year at the University of North Carolina at Chapel Hill. Izzy's father had scraped together every penny he had to send her off. She suspected he'd dipped into his retirement fund despite her protests. Anytime she pressed the subject, he changed the subject.

"You're all I've got, kiddo. Don't worry about me." But she did worry. He was all she had, too. His steady Southern charm was a constant in her life, and she couldn't bear the thought of losing it or letting him down. She worked hard to honor his sacrifices, knowing he'd raised her alone after her mother's death. The last thing she wanted was to burden him with the cost of her dreams.

As a child, Izzy had a knack for solving puzzles—crosswords, number puzzles, and the like. But her favorites were the riddles and mysteries that stumped most people. Able to spot a plot twist from a mile away, Izzy lived to dive into stories that left her reeling. It's what sparked her love for both writing and thrilling mysteries. These loves landed her with a long-felt desire to pursue a career in investigative journalism. With the loss of her mother, her father supported her wholeheartedly.

At UNC, Liam had seemed like the opposite of everything Izzy valued. Where she was grounded, he was carefree, the only son of wealthy real estate moguls. Yet somehow, he'd set his sights on her, the unassuming girl with chestnut hair often tied back in a messy bun. His charm, amplified by his track-star physique and magnetic smile, had initially been irresistible.

Their relationship started with an innocent collision on a jogging path—Liam's orchestrated clumsiness. His flirty apologies and easy confidence were disarming, and before she knew it, he'd worked his way into her life. At first, he'd been attentive and thoughtful, but cracks began to show. His impatience, his selective memory, the way he brushed off her needs as trivial—all signs Izzy had ignored.

With his carefully tousled dark hair, dark piercing eyes, and smile that could melt anyone's defenses, it didn't take long to charm the plain Izzy Reed. His jawline defined and clean-shaven, complemented his lean, muscular body—like the track-stars he hung out with. He flashed a few teasing smiles, showed mild interest in what she was listening to, and soon, she was eating out of his hand. In the beginning, he became everything to her—doting, caring, always carrying her books to class and surprising her with coffee after a long day. *Although, he never remembers how I take my coffee. It's the thought that counts, right?*

Having no frame of reference, what was Izzy to expect? Her only other serious relationship had been with a high school boyfriend. He had broken her heart after cheating on her with a friend. Knowing her love for writing, he even had the gall to ask her for help with his final essay. *I helped him, all right—then congratulated him on his big, fat F. Loser.*

As a result, Izzy didn't go looking for love interests—or casual friendships, for that matter. Too much time and energy wasted on friendships and relationships that end all too quickly. So much effort, wasted. Besides, she had Sophie, her best friend and partner in crime since childhood. They went to school together, spent weekends at each other's houses, and committed to college in Charlotte when the time came.

Though inseparable, they were complementary opposites. While Izzy was reserved and intellectual, Sophie was wild and outgoing. Where Izzy preferred to plan, Sophie leaped without hesitation. Lately, there had been more distance between them than usual, with Sophie heavily involved in her sorority commitments. But Izzy knew Soph would always be there if she needed her, which is why she never asked—or bothered her. *The sorority stuff is so Sophie. She needs this.*

In their senior year, Liam and Izzy lived together in a modest but lovely, two-bedroom apartment. It started casually as a way to "save money" by avoiding the expensive and cramped dorms. Liam had insisted the apartment would allow dogs so her lovable Great Pyrenees mix Marshall—better known as Marshmallow— could live with them. *He knew how much I missed him all the way at my dad's house.* Izzy and her dad had coined the nickname when Marshall was just a puppy. His pure white fur and stout puppy body made him look exactly like, well, a plump marshmallow. And, much like marshmallows in hot cocoa, Izzy found his company far sweeter than most people's.

Sophie had warned Izzy that things with Liam were moving too fast. She worried Izzy was relying on him too much. Izzy had to admit, the apartment and the neighborhood were far beyond what she could afford on her own. But Liam covering more than his share of the rent made it possible. Her residency at the media company didn't exactly pay the bills, at least not like Liam's family money did.

Izzy didn't have the heart to tell Sophie that it was always easier for her—friendships, relationships—even though Sophie went through plenty of them. Living with Liam seemed like a win-win for her. *And I don't have sorority sisters to do everything with.*

Liam and Izzy had their rocky moments, but most of the time, things were… comfortable. She preferred a peaceful routine, unlike Liam, who was always involved in events, meetups, and parties. But most of the time they found a balance between coming and going. Other times… they didn't. He was a bit of a hot head, so it was easier to avoid conflicts than risk the resulting moodiness. And frankly, he was careless with plans, often claiming he *forgot*, that she hadn't specified a day or time like she thought she had, or Izzy's favorite—he was *busy. Like he knows I'll always stay waiting on the back burner. Good 'ol reliable Izzy.* In the end, his charm and easy manner always smoothed over her bitterness, and his assurances of a better tomorrow became a familiar, empty comfort. Rinse and repeat, and a few years passed in the blink of an eye. She stopped bothering to plan, having grown used to not seeing him often. If she were honest, she probably preferred it.

Liam had always been a wild card, living for the next party or exciting event. At first, she didn't mind. She'd spend a few hours at a party with him, then find an excuse to sneak back to her dorm, slip into sweatpants, and dive into a good novel. One hand lost in the world of her book, the other scratching Marshall behind his fuzzy ears. (Sneaking a 105lb dog into her dorm room wasn't an easy task.) No anxiety. No playing *the part*. Just the comfortable peace of another world and conquering someone else's demons. She'd always assumed that the fascination of party life would wear off Liam at some point, and he would back off a touch like most of the students in their later years. But she was still waiting, and if anything, he seemed to have doubled down on his need for the thrill. He'd been going non-stop for so long the dark circles under his eyes were starting to look like a permanent fixture. *He doesn't intend to slow down, either.*

Pregnant.

It seemed she was looking at every detail through the lens of the little life growing inside her. *Will moving too much hurt the baby? Aren't there foods you're not supposed to eat while pregnant? I had that beer two nights ago; did that hurt it...him...her? I hope the leftover Chinese last night wasn't bad.* Feeling permanently altered, her mind, once quiet, now spiraled with worry, threatening to overwhelm her. She placed a steadying hand on her abdomen, trying to calm herself. *Breathe. In. Out.*

First things first. Liam needs to know. Lord, help me.

Izzy felt a wave of panic rise as she heard Liam at the front door of their apartment. She had spent hours wallowing in her shame and doubt, her face puffy from crying. Only once had she considered calling her dad, seeking the comfort of his steady, grounding voice – but the thought of his disappointment stopped her cold. *I can deal with this on my own.*

Izzy's body tensed as Liam's footsteps echoed in the short hallway, each step drawing closer. She inhaled sharply, her fingers gripping the edge of the sofa as she tried to steady the rush of nerves flooding her chest. *Maybe it won't be so bad — maybe he'll be understanding.* His polished shoes landed heavy and abrupt on the wood floor, and she knew the mood he was in without needing to see him.

Marshall, sensing her distress, curled up on the couch beside her, resting his head on her lap. The weight of him was a welcome comfort.

As Liam crossed into the living room, Izzy tucked her legs beneath her, clutching a pillow to her middle as if protecting the little heart beating apart from her own. Neither of them spoke at first, each aware they were on a precipice. They looked at one another, waiting for one to break the silence.

Liam locked eyes with her, adding a sigh of exasperation. "What's wrong, Isabelle?" His tone carried more annoyance than concern. *Oh, how I hate it when he calls me my full name. Like calling me "Izzy" is beneath him.* Her blood pounded in her ears, her heart racing at his tone and the weight of what she was about to reveal. She tried and failed to swallow the lump in her throat. Unable to speak, her trembling hands placed the pregnancy test on the coffee table.

Izzy studied Liam's reddening face with worry as a vein bulged in his temple. She retreated to her protected position in her couched corner, mentally preparing herself for the eruption. *Here it comes.*

"What the hell is that?" Liam snarled, his eyes growing wide.

"It's positive," Izzy choked out through tears. It's all she could manage to say, her throat impossibly tight with emotion.

Liam raked his fingers through his hair, throwing his head back, staring at the ceiling as he paced the small space between couch and kitchen. Izzy remained quiet. She knew all too well that when Liam was provoked, he either exploded or ran. Tonight, she didn't want to push him in either direction, so she let him process the revelation in silence.

After a few moments, Liam said softly, but devoid of sweetness, "How long?"

"Uhm... around eight weeks, I think? When I missed my period, I thought—"

"Not that!" Liam interrupted Izzy's ramblings.

Izzy froze, confused and hurt by Liam's uncaring tone. Marshall's head perked up at the malice in Liam's voice. He lowered his fuzzy head and pulled back his ears as if to say *careful, buddy*.

"How long have you been planning this?" Liam said, his eyes accusing her even more than his words—if that were even possible.

Stunned, Izzy opened her mouth and closed it again as if trying to remember how to speak. Her thoughts struggled for words that wouldn't come. Cocking her head to the side with furrowed eyebrows, all she managed past her stunned lips was a whisper, "What?" Her voice cracked and she paused. "Are you serious?"

Liam didn't move or speak while Izzy's mouth hung open and her breath hitched. He only stared at her with his hands in the pockets of those stupid fine-tailored pants of his. "You won't get anything out of me for this; you know that right?" he said calmly, coldly. *His absolute arrogance!*

The tears dried up within Izzy as her hands shook, a warm, steadying rage replacing the shame and sadness she'd felt only moments ago. The more she realized he truly meant what he said, the more that warmth ignited, turning her blood to boiling. The tops of her ears felt hot, and a strange pressure began building in her forehead as she stared at his face, twisted with so much malice... for her.

"I don't want anything from you." Izzy rallied her strength, drawing in another steadying breath for the babe growing inside her—probably about the size of a raspberry (thank you, internet)—and for herself. For the years she'd lost. Years wasted, spent with this horrible wretch of a man... no, a boy. An immature, selfish boy.

Marshall nuzzled Izzy's hand, and she grounded herself in the reassuring feel of his thick coat. She knew things weren't *great* between them lately, but still, his reaction shocked her. Though he was a hot head, he wasn't typically *cruel* like the guy standing before her now.

The arguing and angry words continued in a blur that felt like hours on end. Through the raised voices and harsh expressions, she wondered if she ever really knew him. Had they become too busy to truly see one another anymore? This was certainly not the same man who had charmed her pants off during their freshman year. Finally, after suggesting that Izzy was, in more polite terms, a gold-digger, she'd had enough. Moments before she could let her rage explode and scream at him, he had the audacity to continue.

"You need to end it," he said with more poison in his voice than she thought he was capable of.

Marshall lowered his head to the couch, letting out a low growl at the words that threatened his Izzy.

"Shut the hell up, Marshall!" Liam shouted.

Marshall looked up at Izzy for confirmation of her well-being as if her opinion was the only one that mattered.

"I can get you an appointment somewhere that will keep it quiet," Liam said. He stood there, gesturing to Izzy and the two lines that had changed everything. He pulled his phone out of his pocket as if he was about to make it all *go away*. Izzy's stomach churned and she felt she might retch at the mere thought.

A mother. Izzy never really knew hers for long due to her illness. She was young—too young for most memories to be distinguished from dreams. Few remained that were tangible enough for her to recall. The sound of her mother's voice was beyond reach. Vaguely, she remembered the smell of freshly baked bread and a flowery perfume, though it remained hazy, unable to come fully into focus. Like a word on the tip of your tongue, just beyond your grasp. The thought saddened her—she couldn't recall hearing her mother's voice express the kind of bonded love already deeply rooted inside her. The next thought had her ready to fight: the idea that this sniveling, selfish man was suggesting this helpless little life might never hear those words from her. Because what? Was it *inconvenient* for him? A protective, primal intensity reared its head. Suddenly, it felt as though Liam had casually suggested ripping the heart right from her chest with a simple "appointment." *I can't. I won't.*

"Get out," Izzy finally said in an angry whisper. This time, her voice shook, not with fear—only adrenaline-encased rage.

Liam looked at her in disbelief for a moment, mouth slack and his eyes narrowed to slits.

"What? I pay for this place, and you expect me to leave?" Liam scoffed.

Izzy didn't reply. She only stared at him with a territorial storm raging in those blue eyes of hers, warning of what lay ahead, should he not listen. She buried her fingers in Marshall's fur to stop him from seeing the fury with which her hands now shook, begging to wring his neck. *Can you even choke a man with no spine?*

After what felt like an eternity of silence, Liam relented, scoffing.

"Fine." He yanked his jacket from the chair where he'd placed it earlier and made for the door. "Figure it out yourself!" he shouted over his shoulder, halfway out the door.

The sound of the door slamming clanged through Izzy like the toll of a bell. And just like that, she was on her own. But she no longer felt like crying. *Good riddance.*

The night Liam left, Izzy didn't reach out to anyone. Each time she picked up the phone to call or text Sophie or her dad, she imagined their responses. Unable to stomach the disappointment in her less-than-perfect choices, she set the phone down each time. She was prepared to figure things out on her own, like Liam had suggested the night before. However, the following day, she was reeling. As she scoured the internet, she quickly realized there was more information on pregnancy than she knew what to do with—advertisements insisting on must-haves, new technology, and breastfeeding versus formula. It was too much for one day, leaving her breathless at times. By evening, she stepped away from searching and came up for air.

Then, as if she'd read her mind, Sophie called. Unaware of the cataclysmic changes in Izzy's life over the last 24 hours, she called to catch up and invite her to yet another sorority soiree for one charity or another. Izzy forced a smile into her voice. She hated turning Sophie down... again. But she also hated the idea of enduring another evening in the sorority scene—fake smiles, endless chatter—even more. It just wasn't *her.*

"It's a white out, Izz. You've always been so elegant in white. Won't you come? It really will be fun; I promise!" Sophie filled Izzy in with more details than she ever cared to know about sorority parties, promising magic, fun, and the like.

Izzy wanted to word-vomit all the events of the last 24 hours into the phone. The words sat on the tip of her tongue as Sophie continued her attempts to convince her. She wanted to scream about what had happened with Liam, to tell Sophie that she needed her, that she couldn't keep up the façade of being put together, *that she missed her.* But Sophie went on about her plans for twinkling lights, the pulsating playlist, the *electric* atmosphere. There was so much joy in her voice as she described it all. Biting her lip, Izzy contemplated whether or not to shatter her friend's twinkly sorority plans with her mess of a life. *I can do this on my own for now. I can tell her about the baby when her twinkly party is done—.*

A sharp knock on the door interrupted Izzy's thoughts. She rose from the bench where she had been perched in the sunlight of the bay window, her favorite spot to read and study, with a view of the stunning cityscape beyond. At the door, she squinted through the peephole, Marshmallow wedged between her and the exit. The distorted image of two uniformed officers appeared. Her heart skipped a beat not knowing what to expect. She felt as if a bucket of cold water had been dumped on her head. Shock, then uncertainty, twisted in her gut. *What could they possibly want?*

"Soph, I'm gonna have to call you back. There's someone at the door." Click. I'm sure she'll give me crap about that later, but at least I didn't have to fight her about the party.

Izzy unlocked the deadbolt and peeked out the door at the two men, her heartbeat quickening in her chest.

"Hi... can I help you?" Izzy managed to ask.

Marshall insisted on surveying the two men with a good sniff. Apparently, deciding they were trustworthy, he demanded the men repay him with head scratches for his spectacular defensive performance.

Izzy's mind reeled expectantly as she studied the two.

"Yes, I'm Officer Jansen, and this is Officer Thomas. Is this the residence of Liam Grager?"

Surprised to hear Liam's name, Izzy wondered what stupidity he'd gotten himself mixed up in. *Probably went out to a party after he left and peed somewhere inappropriate.*

"Yes. I'm his... I mean, we were..." Izzy stammered. *What is he to me now?* "We, uhm, were dating...until yesterday. He lives here. We live... he... he left last night." She internally chastised herself for tripping over her words and added, "Is everything okay?" Her brows furrowed with growing concern.

The officers exchanged a look that had Izzy's stomach in knots. She searched for answers in their gaze. The anxious intensity of the waiting squeezed her chest and threatened to crush her from the inside out. Her mind was blank with the endless possibilities. *PLEASE, spit it out!*

"Uh, ma'am. We recovered his vehicle this afternoon..." The officer paused, looking at her as if the news might break her. He continued, "We got a report of a broken guardrail on the highway up to the lake. Upon inspecting the scene, we found tire marks indicating he may have swerved at a high speed—"

"Oh my gosh... is he okay?!" Izzy struggled to process the rush of conflicting emotions. She still hated Liam for the things he'd said, but that didn't mean she wanted him hurt. Her mind immediately conjured an image of him in a hospital bed, battered and bruised with tubes and wires in and around every surface of his body. Her dinner threatened to make an appearance, and she pressed her belly. *Breathe. In. Out.* The nausea briefly released its grip, but her head began to pound.

"Well, you see, we recovered the vehicle *in* the lake, ma'am." The officer looked at her as if the conversation physically pained him.

Izzy's thoughts took off and left her in the dust as she stared and stared at the officers, not fully comprehending what they had said. *He crashed into Lake Norman?*

When Izzy didn't respond, the officer added. "You should know, ma'am. We haven't recovered the body. We're still searching."

A body. Not Liam. Not his handsome stupid smile. His body.

Izzy struggled to moisten her mouth as she raised her trembling hand to her head. "So, if you're looking for a body... you're assuming, he's..." *dead.* She couldn't bring herself to say it out loud, and she tried to swallow the bile threatening to rise. Her head throbbed as if thoughts were trying to break free of her forehead.

"The hospitals haven't reported any patients matching Liam's description and based on the high speeds indicated by the wreckage and the aerial search coming up dry...." The officers continued to outline how extensive the search had been and assured her their efforts would continue until... Their words trailed off as Izzy lost focus, overwhelmed by her circumstances.

Izzy couldn't reconnect to her surroundings, unable to grasp any of the details of the officer's conversation as her mind begged to escape from the reality before her.

Instead, she thought back to the times they'd boated on Lake Norman, just her and Liam. Those hot, relaxing days in the sun were some of their best. They'd boat on the lake until they were sun-kissed and exhausted, then hike up to stay in his family's cabin deep in the beautiful wilderness of the Blue Ridge Mountains. She still remembered the long hikes through the pine-rich air. Sitting by the gorgeous stone fireplace with hot cider. The crisp, fresh mountain air turned Liam into the peaceful, tuned-in man she had hoped was his true self, and less of the party boy she had come to know. Maybe it had always been a pipe dream to believe he'd been in there somewhere, all along. *Now, she'd never know.*

Izzy gave the officers the various phone numbers they requested, including Liam's parents'. Her heart sank as she imagined these same officers knocking on the Gragers' door. *They'll be devastated.* Part of her wondered if she should call them first, but they'd never been close. The Gragers had wanted *more* than a girl from the backwoods for their son. Maybe that was why Liam chose her in the first place, out of rebellion. Another knot tangled itself deep within her as she thought about the wreck. *It's my fault he left.*

The officers promised to contact Izzy with any new developments in the search, but her mind barely registered their words. Guilt consumed her, manifesting itself as fierce, swarming nausea. And as she closed the door, she turned and hurried to the bathroom. She leaned over the sink and retched again and again.

Three days later, the search for Liam was called off. His body was not found.

Another two weeks passed, and Izzy was awakened by a warm trickle between her legs, slow and deliberate. She sighed deeply and got out of bed for what seemed like the millionth time, assuming she needed to empty her bladder—again. The fullness in her pelvis felt so odd and new, but it also made the pregnancy feel more real. It made her strangely thankful for the discomfort, a reminder that she had turned her life upside down for a tangible, living being. She'd finally seen it for herself at the appointment she'd scheduled last week with an obstetrician in Charlotte. She'd sobbed through heavy breaths, sprawled out on the exam table as she watched the little bean's heart beating on the ultrasound. If they were tears of awe or grief, she wasn't sure. *My baby.*

Izzy went alone, wanting to confirm what she already knew before she revealed her situation to others. She was pregnant, and still too much of a coward to reveal it, especially after what happened to Liam. *God help me, Liam. I'm so sorry.* Every person she'd encountered expressed their concern, unhelpful platitudes, and offered to be there *if she needed anything.* She couldn't bear the thought of the pitiful looks she'd receive if anyone knew she was carrying her dead boyfriend's baby. These weeks had been filled with regret for fighting with him. If only she hadn't made him leave—not to bring him back, but to spare him from whatever horror he'd endured that night. *If it weren't for me, he might be alive.*

The recurring thoughts and guilt followed her in her sleepy haze as she walked to the bathroom. But as she sat on the toilet, the world seemed to tilt on its axis as she looked down at the carnage beneath her. The warm trickle she'd felt was blood—bright crimson, stark against the white porcelain and her olive skin. It stained the seat and her legs in a mockingly bright hue. The pain began shortly after—sharp, piercing, deep in her core. She clutched her abdomen, horror settling over her, cold and unforgiving. *No. No. No. I can come up with a plan. I can do this on my own, please, God. No.*

Since seeing her baby's heart beat, Izzy's bond, already deep and impenetrable had grown stronger. Now, the life she had felt inside her was slipping away uncontrollably like liquid through her fingers. She was powerless to quench whatever had burst forth within her. *Too much blood, too much pain.* With every gush, every crushing pang, a haunting emptiness settled inside her, knowing she was helpless to change it. She couldn't stop it from leaving her body, no longer hers to nurture. She sobbed, screamed, and prayed, but it didn't stop, no matter how desperately she begged.

Slowly, she lowered herself into the bathtub of her silent, empty apartment. The hot water streamed down her back as she sat with her knees to her chest. Her gaze fixated on the twisted trail of red as it washed into the drain. After fumbling to find the number to the OB doctor on-call, her trembling fingers barely managed to dial. When the voice on the other end finally answered, their words only confirmed what she had already suspected. *There's not much to do. If the bleeding is too much, go to the Emergency Room. We'll follow up next week. I'm so sorry.* Izzy knew by the sound of the woman's voice that her baby was gone. She had no idea how much time had passed under the water's calming embrace. Her only anchor to time was that fuzzy white nose pushing past the shower curtain to check and see if she was okay. *No, buddy, I'm not.*

Izzy forced herself off the shower floor, each movement a slow, painful effort. She prepared her clothes for the continued torrent of blood as she dressed for bed. The sharp cramping in her abdomen was relentless, unlike anything she'd ever felt. She tucked herself back into the thick covers, making room for a near-frantic Marshall beneath the layers. He must've sensed her discomfort and heartbreak because he moved quickly as if he meant to fix her somehow, to put her back together, if she would only place the pieces in his paws. Half of his body weight pressed across her abdomen as he lay his head on her chest, looking up at her with concern. His body remained still, but his perceptive eyes searched her face for a solution.

"I think our little buddy is gone, Marsh," Izzy said sobbing, her eyes already swollen with grief. He didn't move his head from her as his ears perked up, and his head tilted, trying to understand. Izzy's voice was thick with sorrow, the words breaking through her tears as she spoke. "It's just me and you again, buddy," she said faintly. Marshall seemed to understand her meaning and sighed deeply as they both drifted off into a fitful sleep.

CHAPTER 2

NOW

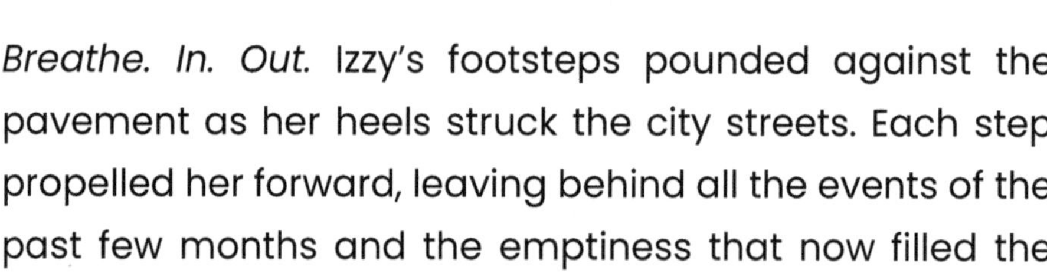

Breathe. In. Out. Izzy's footsteps pounded against the pavement as her heels struck the city streets. Each step propelled her forward, leaving behind all the events of the past few months and the emptiness that now filled the silence of her days. She relished the physical burn—the distraction it provided. Marshall zoomed alongside her, his tongue lolling out of the side of his mouth as he ran. *Good for you, buddy. Someone ought to be enjoying themselves.*

"Sail" by AWOLNATION blasted in Izzy's ears, the aggressive bass beat reverberating in her chest. She leaned into the physical burn, using it as a distraction from the gnawing emptiness that greeted her each morning. The ache in her thighs and the thudding of her heart were welcome counterpoints to the pain she couldn't escape.

Izzy loved this city with its modern, sleek edges woven into historic charm. The ancient stone complemented the glass skyscrapers that reached toward the clouds, reflecting the golden sunrise as she passed them in a blur. *Breathe. In. Out.* Her mind began wandering back to the anchor of her grief. In her mind's eye, flashes of red blood covered her legs and hands. Anguish threatened to creep in. The crisp morning air filled her lungs as she pushed herself harder. Her thighs burned, and her feet ached with every footfall – she relished in the diversion. *Breathe. In. Out.*

Around her, Izzy's eyes were drawn to pockets of trees. They reminded her of her childhood spent amongst the forested mountains, the grounding peace that she'd felt. She borrowed a kernel of the feeling from her memory. The intensity of the summer sun lingered, beating down on her shoulders as she navigated the streets. Sweat trailed down her spine as she continued to push her body to its limits.

Marshall paused to sniff a lamppost, and managed to rustle up a few of the first fallen leaves that sprinkled the manicured grass. The city bustled all around her, alive with motion. Despite it, she'd always found serenity here. But lately, it felt different—like everything was moving on without her. She tried to ground herself in the ordinary. The routines. But lately, she felt she was running. From all of it—the anger, the loss, the guilt... the loneliness.

What truly unsettled her spirit was the disconnect she now felt, like a ghost floating through what was left of Izzy's life. No one knew how she truly suffered, how she was tortured by the moments she'd awakened in the night. By that fleeting second when she'd forget the grief, only for it to return in an earth-shattering wave, like a smothering, unrelenting fog. It was the feeling that no one fully understood her—the scope of her anguish and the rollercoaster of emotions that fueled it. Yet, how could she be understood, revealing her truth, without the weight of their disappointment adding another burden to her shoulders? *I already have too much to carry.*

The beat in her ears ceased abruptly as a call came through her headphones. Izzy slowed her pace, seeing "Pops" on the screen brought a pang of guilt. She paused the music, letting the silence settle as she answered.

"Hey, Pops, how's it going?" she asked, forcing brightness into her voice. *Put on the mask, Izz.* Her heartbeat was loud in her ears, from the intensity of her run and the fear that he might catch on to her ruse.

Her father's drawl came through the line, "Hey there, darlin'. Just wanted to check in. Haven't heard from you in a few days. You doing okay?"

Izzy's smile faltered. She hated lying to him, but the truth felt too heavy. "Yeah, I'm good. On a run with Marshall, like you said."

"That's my girl. Tough as nails, Izz. Always have been," he said warmly. Izzy couldn't help the plume in her chest at the familiar sentiment.

Yet, her throat tightened at the things she caged, unshared. She longed to tell him everything—about Liam, the pregnancy, the loss. But she couldn't bear the thought of seeing disappointment in his eyes. She swallowed, "Thanks Dad. I'm gonna finish this run and then I've got to head back. I need to get back to studying for finals." The lie sat rancid on her tongue as she tried to hurry the conversation along – her finals already done for the semester. *He wouldn't understand. He'd only be hurt, because I'm hurting. He's been through enough.*

"Okay, darlin'. I'll let ya go, I love ya. Make time to come hang out with your old man next week, yeah?" His voice was laced with longing and worry.

"Yeah, Dad. I'll do my best. Love you," her voice soft, they hung up. Her remorse was heavy – she knew he was lonely. *I have enough things to feel guilty about right now.*

Her legs felt leaden and wobbly as she trotted back up the final steps to her apartment building, Marshall panting deeply beside her. She managed to get the key into the lock before noticing a sheet of paper taped to her front door. She pushed her headphones down onto her neck, her jaw dropping in disbelief as she read what was written.

"NORTH CAROLINA EVICTION NOTICE

This notice is sent to ISABELLE REED (Tenant) and further directed to all residents, occupants, and subtenants therein."

Izzy's breath quickened as the ground seemed to slip from beneath her. Sitting on the top step, she struggled to read the notice through the panic that threatened to consume her.

"In accordance with your Lease Agreement and the laws of North Carolina....

you have been found in NONPAYMENT. Within 10 days, the Landlord demands the

total amount due, including all late fees, service fees, and charges, totaling: $5000

Failure to make the above payment within the required time frame will result in termination of the aforementioned Lease Agreement. The Tenant, listed above, will be required to vacate and deliver possession of premises within 30 days of this notice."

Izzy closed her eyes, her gut twisting with the sharp sting of shame that settled deep in her belly. She couldn't believe it—not after everything that had happened to her—that this was where she was now. *Homeless. Breathe. In. Out. I can fix this. I have to.*

Izzy dialed the number for the apartment manager. Sandra answered on the second ring, as if she had been expecting Izzy's call.

"Izzy, I know—" Sandra attempted to explain.

"No, I don't think you understand, Sandra. You see, I'm confused. I have this notice on my door saying I'm about to be homeless when I *know* we discussed that you'd give me 30 days to come up with half. *Ten days?!*" Izzy was harsh, angrier than poor, sweet Sandra deserved. Izzy knew it. She couldn't help the anger welling up inside her, boiling over at the thought of what a pitiful story her life had become.

When it rains, it pours?! *Well, I'd better buckle up, cause the storm clouds are rolling and it's starting to hail for heaven's sake.*

"I'm so sorry, dear. With everything that happened to sweet Liam, I thought the owner would honor that agreement. Especially considering their affiliation with the Grager family... but they insisted that the standard lease terms had to be honored." She paused, and when Izzy didn't respond, she added, "I'm just so sorry, dear. My hands are tied. You understand?"

Breathe. In. Out.

At the mention of Liam and his parents defeat won out, and the giant bubble that, a moment ago, had felt like it would burst, deflated along with her will to fight. "I get it, Sandra. Thanks for trying." Izzy supposed her coldness was better than her rage, and she hung up. She couldn't bring herself to bother with the pleasantries of a goodbye. *I've had too many goodbyes lately.*

Marshall rested his heavy head on her knees, and she rubbed his ears. She laid her forehead gently on his head and sighed deeply into the silence. *What now?*

CHAPTER 3

IZZY

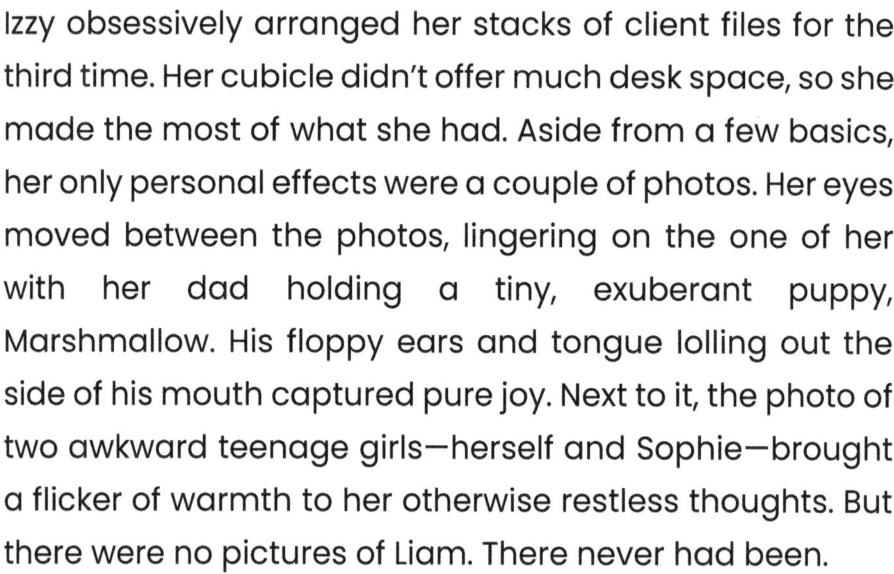

Izzy obsessively arranged her stacks of client files for the third time. Her cubicle didn't offer much desk space, so she made the most of what she had. Aside from a few basics, her only personal effects were a couple of photos. Her eyes moved between the photos, lingering on the one of her with her dad holding a tiny, exuberant puppy, Marshmallow. His floppy ears and tongue lolling out the side of his mouth captured pure joy. Next to it, the photo of two awkward teenage girls—herself and Sophie—brought a flicker of warmth to her otherwise restless thoughts. But there were no pictures of Liam. There never had been.

The realization stung more than she expected, stirring a wave of guilt. Everyone spoke kindly of him now, their sympathetic comments weighing on her like a stone. Yet, she had no visual reminder of him to remove, no cherished memories immortalized in glossy prints. She forced herself to shake it off and opened her email, scanning the list of unread messages until her eyes locked on one from her manager.

"Good morning,

Please meet me in my office at 9:30 AM regarding the Brewed Awakening files.

Thank you,

Janice"

Izzy stared at the Blue Horizon Media logo at the bottom of the email, her stomach tightening. What could this meeting be about? Her heart pounded as dread clawed its way into her chest. She'd been an intern at Blue Horizon for nearly two years, pouring her energy into earning a real position in their journalism division. The internship was paid, but the modest salary barely covered her expenses. *Obviously, according to the note on my door.* While most of her work involved mundane tasks, she'd occasionally been able to contribute to campaign designs for rising clients. She took pride in those moments, showcasing her writing skills and earning praise for her creativity. Lately, though, she'd been slipping. Her once-sharp focus had dulled, replaced by foggy thoughts and a frustrating inability to meet her usual standards.

And now, she remembered.

The Brewed Awakening files.

Her chest tightened as the realization hit like a sucker punch. The deadline had passed last week. She'd promised to complete the social media strategy, a project she had once been excited about. Brewed Awakening was everything she admired—a coffee company rooted in sustainability, blending affordability with biodegradable packaging. They'd even extended her deadline after news of Liam's accident spread. It had been a gesture of kindness she hadn't deserved.

"I've got this," she had told them. But she hadn't.

The shame was unbearable. She'd fought so hard for a chance to prove herself, and now her dreams of advancing as a journalist seemed to be slipping through her fingers. All she had worked for—her future—felt like it was unraveling, one missed deadline at a time.

Izzy tugged nervously at the hem of her pencil skirt, wishing it reached a little lower. The chairs in Janice's office were set awkwardly far back from the desk, leaving her feeling exposed and vulnerable. Outwardly, she projected calm, poised professionalism. Inside, though, she yearned for a shield—anything to soften the blow she was bracing for.

Janice's assistant had shown her in promptly at 9:30, offering a polite but pitying smile that Izzy barely managed to return. She knew Janice was making her wait deliberately. Sure, Izzy had messed up, but she didn't need the theatrics. *Trust me; no one will punish me more than myself.*

The office door opened, and Janice walked in with her signature briskness, a steaming cup of coffee in hand. She settled into her oversized chair, took a sip, and winced slightly at the heat. Her eyes flicked briefly to Izzy, and she set the cup down with a deliberate motion. *Here it comes.*

"How are you, Isabelle?" Janice's tone was warm, but the pity in her gaze sent a fresh wave of heat to Izzy's cheeks. Sympathy. She could handle anger, scolding, or even outright dismissal. But the sympathy made her feel small.

Yell at me; fire me, anything. Just don't LOOK at me like that.

"I'm okay, Janice. Thanks for asking." Izzy forced herself to meet her manager's eyes, clasping her hands tightly to keep them from fidgeting. "Look, Janice, I realize this is about the coffee account... I really messed up, and I'm so sorry. I've already started working on the portfolio report this morning, and—"

Janice raised a hand to cut her off. "Yes, yes, yes. I'm sure it was a simple oversight. I *do* need those reports, but I've already asked Mark to familiarize himself with your client list so you can take some time to focus on your personal life." She smiled as if she'd just given Izzy the gift of a lifetime. "You've been through a lot recently, and given your history of excellent work for us, I figured you could use a little help."

Izzy froze. *Help? She thinks I can't handle these accounts.* "While I appreciate it, I really don't think that's necessary," she said quickly. I'm sure Mark has plenty of accounts he could be handling. I promise I won't let it happen again." Her heel tapped an anxious rhythm against the carpet. *Please. I can't take anything else right now.*

"Isabelle," Janice said firmly, though her smile didn't waver. "I know the work you're capable of. But given everything you've been through, I want to make sure you're supported. Mark's cleared his schedule to help, so you can take a little time during fall break to reset. It's a win-win."

The finality in Janice's tone left no room for argument. Izzy nodded stiffly, murmuring the appropriate pleasantries before excusing herself.

She slumped back into her desk chair, staring blankly at the glowing screen in front of her. She knew Janice meant well. She truly appreciated the slack being cut for her. But all she could feel was shame, the gnawing certainty that she'd failed. *Pull it together, Izzy. You're slipping.*

CHAPTER 4

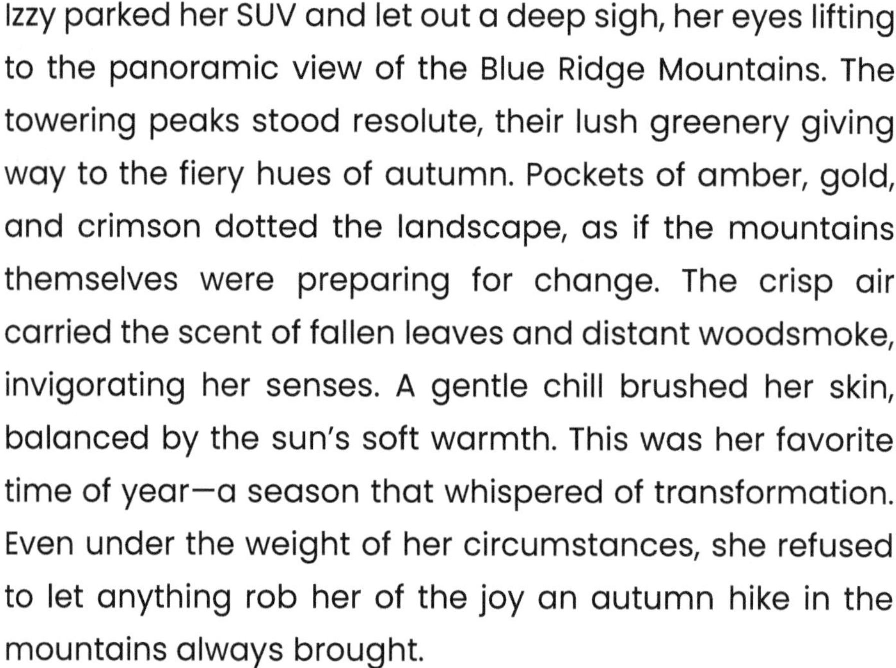

Izzy parked her SUV and let out a deep sigh, her eyes lifting to the panoramic view of the Blue Ridge Mountains. The towering peaks stood resolute, their lush greenery giving way to the fiery hues of autumn. Pockets of amber, gold, and crimson dotted the landscape, as if the mountains themselves were preparing for change. The crisp air carried the scent of fallen leaves and distant woodsmoke, invigorating her senses. A gentle chill brushed her skin, balanced by the sun's soft warmth. This was her favorite time of year—a season that whispered of transformation. Even under the weight of her circumstances, she refused to let anything rob her of the joy an autumn hike in the mountains always brought.

Marshall bolted from the backseat like a shot, his tail wagging furiously. Izzy smiled as she grabbed her pack, watching him conduct his usual patrol of the area. His excitement was infectious, a reminder of simpler times. As she stuffed her supplies into the pack's pockets, she glanced at Marshall, now engrossed in sniffing a patch of grass. *Maybe the rest is what I need after all.*

She clipped her 9mm Beretta Cheetah into the holster on her hip. Encounters with predators were rare but not unheard of. It was always better to be prepared. Marshall returned from his reconnaissance mission, his paws dancing with anticipation as she secured his leash to his collar. Together, they turned to the trail—a familiar sanctuary that had always offered her solace.

These mountains were more than just a place to hike. After her mother died, her dad had brought her here on hunting trips, unsure of how else to raise a young girl on his own. Those weekends became their unspoken language of healing. While they rarely talked about their grief, the silence of the woods seemed to say enough. Her dad taught her to respect the land, to identify plants, and to handle a gun safely. She absorbed it all with a determination to make him proud. And she did.

The mountains had become her escape—a place where she felt grounded, capable, and free.

As they walked the trail, Izzy's thoughts, carefully walled off for weeks, began to seep through. At first, they were faint, like whispers on the wind. Then they surged forward, relentless and loud.

I screwed up that account at work. They don't trust me anymore. I'll never be a journalist if I can't prove myself. I'm going to lose the apartment. I can't afford it without Liam, and I sure as hell can't afford a new place without a job.

Liam's gone. And it's my fault.

I shouldn't have provoked him into leaving. I should've kept calm. But then... the baby. My baby. My baby...

Her chest tightened as the familiar ache resurfaced. It was a chasm, a deep, endless void that swallowed everything else. She'd read about the stages of grief—acceptance, moving forward—but how could she accept this? How could she let go of something so innocent, so miraculous, that had been taken from her?

The weight of it pressed down, and her breath came in uneven gasps. She tried to hold it in, to keep herself together, but the tears spilled over. The vibrant colors of the forest blurred as her vision clouded, and her sobs broke the silence. She let it happen here, in the one place she didn't have to be strong. Here, alone but not lonely, she allowed herself to unravel. She wouldn't do it in front of others—not with their pitying looks, their murmured platitudes. She couldn't.

After what felt like hours but was only minutes, Izzy took a deep, shaky breath and wiped her face. *Just keep going.* And she did. Step by step, she moved forward, her breathing evening out with each stride. The fresh air filled her lungs and cleared her mind, offering a whisper of something she hadn't felt in a long time: hope.

The feeling drove her to pray, something she hadn't done in years. Her words were halting and raw, a mixture of rage, despair, and desperation. She brought it all—the weariness from pretending she wasn't breakable, the shattered pieces of herself she'd tried so hard to hide. Surely the God who parted seas could handle her brokenness.

As she walked, her eyes stayed fixed on the trail, the trees, the endless sky. The only sounds were the crunch of leaves underfoot, the rustle of the wind, and Marshall's steady breathing beside her. And for the first time in what felt like forever, she let herself believe she might be okay.

The sharp snap of a twig shattered the forest's stillness, the sound reverberating like a gunshot in the quiet. Izzy froze mid-step, her head whipping toward the source of the noise as her pulse quickened. She moved cautiously up the incline, her breath shallow, straining to hear over the pounding of her own heartbeat.

For a moment, the silence pressed down on her, thick and oppressive. Then another rustle—closer this time—broke through the stillness. She glanced at Marshall. His body was rigid, head low, ears pricked, his entire frame tuned to the unseen threat. A low growl rumbled from deep within his chest, reverberating into the shadows of the trees.

Izzy swallowed hard, her instincts flaring. Marshall was rarely like this. They were in sync enough that she trusted his reactions implicitly. Something—or someone—was watching them.

The hair on the back of her neck stood on end, her body humming with adrenaline. She casually dropped Marshall's leash, trusting him to stay close. Her eyes darted across the dense forest, scanning for any movement. Slowly, she eased open the clasp on her hip holster. Her fingers curled around the grip of her pistol, drawing it out inch by inch. The weight of the weapon was reassuring, a solid, familiar presence in her trembling hands.

A cold sweat prickled along her forehead, and she blinked it away, her senses razor-sharp. Marshall let out a single, sharp bark, his teeth bared now, the growl escalating into a warning. Izzy adjusted her stance, her grip tightening as she braced herself.

Leaves rustled, twigs cracked underfoot, and the underbrush trembled as something massive moved into view. A sob caught in her throat as the largest black bear she'd ever seen emerged from behind the trees. Its sheer size stole the breath from her lungs.

Izzy pulled the slide of her pistol back to chamber a round, the mechanical click jarring against the natural sounds of the forest. Her whispered prayer was frantic, raw. *Please, God, don't let me have to use this.*

Izzy's thoughts raced, a flood of memories crashing into her as she recalled the countless lessons her dad had drilled into her about predators in these mountains. Her pistol—his gift—was a reminder of those lessons, of his insistence that she not only carry it but know how to use it effectively. He had ensured she was trained, even lethal if it came to that.

One memory surfaced, sharp and vivid. It was a cool autumn morning, years ago, when they had shared a hunting stand deep in these woods. A young, curious black bear had wandered too close, scaling the tree beside them with surprising agility. Izzy could still feel the tremble in her limbs, the uncontrollable shaking as adrenaline surged through her veins.

The bear had climbed higher, its dark eyes locking onto hers. She had been paralyzed, face-to-face with its large black snout, the musky scent of its fur mingling with the crisp mountain air. Her father's voice had come low and steady in her ear, a tether to reason amidst her panic.

"Stay very still," he had whispered. "Start to spread your arms out, make yourself big. He's just curious, darlin'. That's right. Good."

Her father had been right. Slowly, the bear had lost interest, turning and retreating down the tree as if the encounter had been nothing more than a passing curiosity. They had spent hours afterward talking about black bears, her dad patiently explaining their solitary nature, their preference to avoid conflict unless provoked.

That moment had stayed with her, a testament to her father's calm under pressure and the profound respect he had taught her for these creatures. Now, standing in the shadow of the present, she clung to that memory like a lifeline, willing herself to channel his steady confidence.

No, this bear wasn't curious. It stood tall on its hind legs, its roar echoing through the trees and rattling Izzy to her core. Her breath hitched, her pulse pounding in her ears. *Breathe. In. Out. What did I miss? Why is it so angry?*

Izzy shifted her stance, raising her arms to make herself appear larger—just as her dad had taught her. She didn't want to shoot this magnificent creature unless there was no other choice. Her hands trembled as she held the gun, the cold metal grounding her in the chaos of the moment.

Then she saw it. Out of the corner of her eye, two tiny black shapes scrambled through the underbrush, clumsy and panicked. Cubs.

The realization hit her like a jolt of electricity. *She's a mother.* A surge of empathy coursed through Izzy, and her grip on the weapon loosened. The bear wasn't attacking out of malice—it was defending its young, doing whatever it took to protect the fragile lives entrusted to it.

Izzy's gaze returned to the bear as it roared again, swiping the air with claws that could shred bark like paper. Slowly, deliberately, Izzy lowered her gun and slid it back into the holster. Marshall, still bristling with tension, glanced up at her for reassurance.

"It's okay, buddy," she murmured, her voice low and steady. "She's a mama."

Marshall gave a soft whine, his eyes darting back to the bear. Izzy began to back away, her movements slow and measured, each step deliberate. *Step. Step. Step.* Marshall followed, his head turning constantly to keep the massive bear in sight.

The bear dropped to all fours, her sharp eyes fixed on Izzy and Marshall as she sniffed the air, ensuring the threat was retreating. Then, with a slow, deliberate gait, the enormous black creature crossed the trail, reuniting with her cubs.

Izzy's chest tightened as she watched the tiny cubs tumble toward their mother, their cries muffled by the underbrush.

Relief flooded her as the family disappeared into the shadows of the forest. The bear paused once, glancing back at Izzy.

Those black eyes locked onto hers, and for a moment, time seemed to stand still. A quiet understanding passed between them—an unspoken acknowledgment shared from one mother to another.

Izzy exhaled, the weight of the encounter lifting as she turned and continued down the trail. Marshall padded along beside her, his tension slowly easing.

She left the woods feeling lighter than she had in a long, long time.

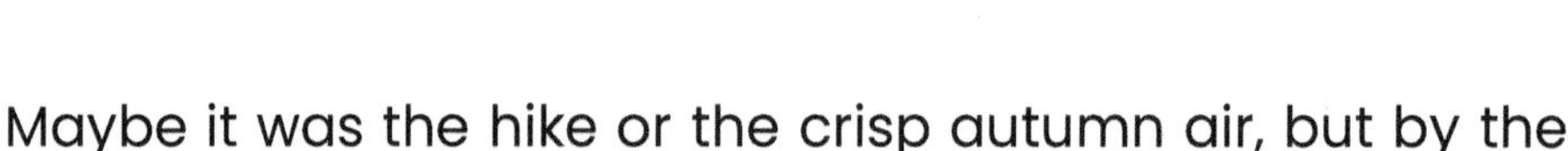

Maybe it was the hike or the crisp autumn air, but by the time Sophie called that evening, Izzy was ready to listen.

"I never see you anymore, and I know I've been busy with sorority stuff... but you're still my best friend, Izz. I wish you'd let me in." Sophie's voice was soft but insistent, the concern woven through her words cutting through Izzy's usual defenses.

Sophie was right. Izzy had been keeping her distance, afraid her darkness would overshadow Sophie's light. Izzy bit her lip, closing her eyes as she searched for a way to begin.

"I know, Soph. I'm sorry," Izzy said quietly. "I've just been... trying to keep it together. Everyone expects me to carry on like nothing's changed, but it's hard. I don't know how to do this."

Even as she spoke, Izzy was surprised by the vulnerability slipping past her carefully constructed walls. It was more than she'd shared with anyone—not even Sophie. On the other end of the line, her friend remained silent, intentionally giving Izzy the space to continue. *Or maybe she's afraid to scare me back into my shell.*

Izzy took a shaky breath, her voice trembling. "Soph, the night of Liam's accident... I didn't tell you everything."

The words hung heavy in the air, and Izzy winced, bracing herself for Sophie's reaction. She could already imagine the hurt and betrayal in her friend's voice: *You're my best friend, how could you keep this from me?!*

But Sophie's response was measured, gentle. "What do you mean, Izz? You know you can tell me anything."

Breathe. In. Out.

So, Izzy did.

Piece by piece, she began to unload. She told Sophie about the pregnancy, her initial panic, and Liam's cold insistence on ending it. She described the tiny heartbeat she'd seen on the monitor and the surge of wonder she'd felt knowing her body could create life. Her voice broke as she recounted waking to the bloody mess, the loss that had hollowed her out, leaving her to carry on as if it hadn't mattered.

Sophie stayed quiet, save for the occasional gasp or the soft sniffle of shared tears. Encouraged by her friend's silence, Izzy continued. She confessed her struggles at work, her fear of losing the apartment, and even the prayer she'd whispered in the woods. She told Sophie about the bear, the strange encounter that left her with a glimmer of hope she hadn't felt in months.

By the time she finished, her voice was hoarse, and her chest felt lighter, as if releasing the words had peeled away a layer of her grief. She sighed deeply. "So... yeah."

"I can't believe Liam would say all that! What an absolute—" Sophie launched into a string of curses so colorful they would have made a sailor blush.

Izzy couldn't help but laugh, a sound she hadn't made in what felt like forever. "Soph! You can't say that!"

"Why not? Because he's dead? Sorry, but that's no excuse. Afterlife or no, he's still a bum." Sophie's bluntness was as sharp as ever, and it was exactly what Izzy needed. Her friend's indignation helped loosen the fingers of guilt clinging to her, if only a little.

With a quiet chuckle, Izzy sighed. "Thanks, Soph. I needed that."

"You need to stop shutting me out," Sophie replied, her tone softening. "A few of the girls and I are going out for drinks tonight, and you're coming with us. Don't even think about making excuses—I'm not taking no for an answer."

Izzy hesitated but knew Sophie was serious. The walls she'd hidden behind had cracked, and there was no retreating now. *Honesty is harder but less lonely, I suppose.*

"Fine," Izzy relented. "But if it's boring, I'm bailing to finish my book with Marshall."

At the sound of his name, Marshall perked up, his ears swiveling toward Izzy. She smiled, scratching his head. *Good boy.*

"I'd expect nothing less," Sophie teased. "I'm coming over now to help you figure out what to wear."

Before Izzy could protest, Sophie hung up. Izzy could already picture her friend arriving in a flurry, coffee in hand

and a warm embrace that, if Izzy were honest, she desperately needed.

A smile—light and unfamiliar—crept across her lips. *Maybe a night out is exactly what I need.*

Izzy's chestnut hair cascaded down in long, bouncy waves, her lips painted a bold burgundy that matched the confidence she wished she felt. The little black dress she wore—the only one she owned—hugged her curves in all the right places. Sophie had insisted she buy it during their freshman year, proclaiming it a "life necessity."

But as Izzy shifted uncomfortably, longing for the comfort of her thrifted sweatpants or yoga pants, she admitted that tonight, she felt beautiful. Maybe even desirable. Did it change how out of place she felt? Only slightly. This scene was never her thing and never would be.

Uptown Charlotte buzzed with life, neon lights reflecting in puddles left behind by the day's pop-up showers. Music and laughter spilled onto the streets from bars, restaurants, and clubs, each venue offering its unique flavor of nightlife. Couples enjoyed quiet dinners to the backdrop of soft, live music, while sports bars erupted with camaraderie and shouts over the latest game. Izzy glanced down at her heels. *At least they get to wear jeans and a ballcap.*

Predictably, Sophie and her Delta Omega Chi sisters had chosen a nightclub: "The Ridge Runner," a flashy homage to Appalachian moonshiners. After fussing over Izzy's outfit, makeup, and hair for what felt like hours, Sophie had summoned their SwiftRide chariot. As the car stopped at the Epicenter's entrance, Izzy took a steadying breath and stepped onto the damp sidewalk, her heels clicking against the wet concrete.

The Epicenter was a hub of activity, housing everything from cafés to boutiques. The crisp night air carried a slight chill, and the first stars twinkled in the darkening sky above. The neon glow of *The Ridge Runner's* sign drew them in, its pulsing lights and throbbing music growing louder with each step.

Inside, the atmosphere was chaotic and electric, colorful lights slicing through the dim interior. Izzy scanned the crowd as they made their way to a table Sophie's friends had claimed. Her eyes swept over the bar—and stopped.

One face stood out, watching them intently. Izzy wasn't a stranger to a man's gaze when she dressed like this, but something about this one felt different. His sandy brown hair was neatly styled, his chiseled features almost too perfect. Attractive, sure, but it wasn't admiration in his eyes. His stare was sharp, intense—hungry.

A shiver crawled up her spine, and she bristled instinctively. She told herself she was overreacting. *Calm down, Izzy. It's just a look.*

Sophie leaned in and shouted over the music, "I see them! Over by the center wall!"

Izzy followed Sophie's lead, weaving through the throng of bodies. The table wasn't tucked away in a cozy corner like she'd hoped but sat squarely in the middle of the action. It divided the bar from the dance floor, putting them on full display.

Five women greeted them at the table, each impossibly beautiful. They clinked shot glasses and downed something golden and syrupy as Izzy approached. Their perfection felt almost uncanny: meticulously styled hair in various shades, tight dresses that clung like a second skin, flawless makeup, manicured French tips, and impossibly white smiles.

Izzy fought the urge to quip about *dining with real-life Barbies*. Instead, she bit her tongue and let Sophie handle the introductions.

As Sophie chatted, Izzy studied her friend. She was different from these women. Sophie's beauty was softer, more natural, her charm effortless. Where the others seemed to scream, "I try hard!" Sophie was magnetic without trying at all.

Izzy felt a pang of guilt. She'd resented Sophie's bond with the sorority girls, assuming her friend fit seamlessly into their world of charity galas and networking soirées. But now, seeing them side by side, the differences were stark. Sophie was unmistakably herself, and that was why they'd always worked so well together.

The truth hit her hard. *They're lucky to have her. Because I am, too.*

After an hour of chatter at the table, covering fundraisers, charity events, and sorority goals, Izzy already felt her social battery draining. Sophie patted her thigh excitedly as the conversation turned to rating the male patrons on the dance floor. Izzy managed a polite smile, chuckling softly at the jokes.

She wasn't holding onto feelings for Liam that would stop her from moving on, but the messiness of it all still haunted her. His accident had laid bare truths she couldn't ignore about who he really was. Even if she wanted to, she couldn't excuse his actions just because he was gone. But tonight wasn't about finding a companion. It wasn't about finding anything at all.

Sophie's warm hand squeezed her arm gently, her soft gaze meeting Izzy's. Without a word, her eyes seemed to say, *I don't have any expectations. I'm just glad we're together.*

Me too, Izzy thought, offering a small, genuine smile in return. For the first time in a long time, she remembered how in sync they could be. She'd missed this—missed Sophie and the quiet understanding they shared.

Conversations ebbed and flowed as trays of colorful, fruity drinks arrived at the table. Izzy, still nursing her whiskey and soda, swirled the last of the liquid in her glass. She rarely drank anymore, and even this felt like enough. The memory of her first and only wild college party lingered in her mind—a night she'd trusted Liam to have her back. Instead, she'd ended up stumbling barefoot back to her dorm, his voicemail taunting her with every unanswered call.

She'd learned her lesson. Never again would she allow herself to lose control like that. Tonight would be no exception. Two drinks, plenty of water, and a clear mind. *Thank you very much.*

Suddenly, he was there—the man from the bar. Izzy startled, drawing in a sharp breath as he appeared beside her at the end of the booth. She'd chosen this spot for its easy escape, but now it felt more like a trap. His sandy brown hair was still perfectly styled, and his tailored shirt and gleaming watch exuded wealth.

"I noticed you might need another," he said, motioning to the server as a fresh whiskey and soda appeared in front of her. His voice was smooth, almost practiced, and his smile revealed unnervingly perfect teeth.

He held out a hand, the gesture almost imperious. "C'mon. Let's dance."

It wasn't a question. Izzy's stomach turned.

Her cheeks flushed as the women at the table looked at her expectantly. The Izzy from two years ago would've been flattered, jumping at the chance. But something about this man felt wrong. *I can't put my finger on it...*

She opened her mouth to politely decline. "I... uh..."

"My darling friend isn't feeling well, but I'd be happy to take you up on that offer," Sophie interrupted smoothly. She slid past Izzy, taking the man's hand before downing a few gulps of the drink he'd brought. Her dazzling smile was disarming as always.

Izzy began to protest. "Soph, you don't ha—"

"Really, Izz, it's fine. I'll catch a ride with the girls. Go home to your sweatpants and give Marshmallow a kiss for me." Sophie planted a kiss on Izzy's cheek, winked, and led the man to the dance floor with a carefree bounce in her step.

He's probably a nice, normal guy—even if he gives me the creeps.

Izzy turned to the other women. "You'll make sure she gets home, right?"

"Of course!" the blonde replied, her voice cheerfully slurred. "Delta Omega Chi sisters stick together, babe!"

Izzy bit back a retort and instead nodded, draining the rest of her drink and her water before opening the SwiftRide app. Her driver was 25 minutes away. Sipping the rest of the whiskey and soda. *At least it's a free drink.*

The minutes crawled as Izzy scrolled through her phone, her interest waning. Occasionally, she glanced at Sophie, still swaying on the dance floor, her hand in the air, the sandy-haired man hovering nearby. Sophie caught her eye and gave her a thumbs-up, her smile as easy as ever. *I'm good. Thanks for coming,* she seemed to say.

Satisfied, Izzy waved one last time and pushed her way toward the door. The cool night air hit her as she stepped outside, the stars scattered above in the crisp autumn sky. She paused, tilting her head back to take them in.

When she lowered her gaze, the ground seemed to tilt. She blinked hard, shaking her head to clear the haze. *Two drinks, plenty of water. Why do I feel so off?*

Her heels clicked faintly as she crossed the atrium, but with each step, her legs grew heavier. A leaden sensation spread through her body, and her surroundings blurred.

Panic clawed at the edges of her mind. Something wasn't right.

She stumbled to the curb, fumbling with her phone. *Five minutes. Just five minutes.* Her fingers felt clumsy as she typed, her vision swimming. "Pleasee hurry." She hit send, hoping it was enough.

Her heart raced as darkness crept into her periphery. She sank onto the curb, her head swimming. The wet concrete chilled her skin, but her awareness slipped further.

The last sound she registered was the screech of tires and hurried footsteps approaching before the world went black.

CHAPTER 6

GABRIEL

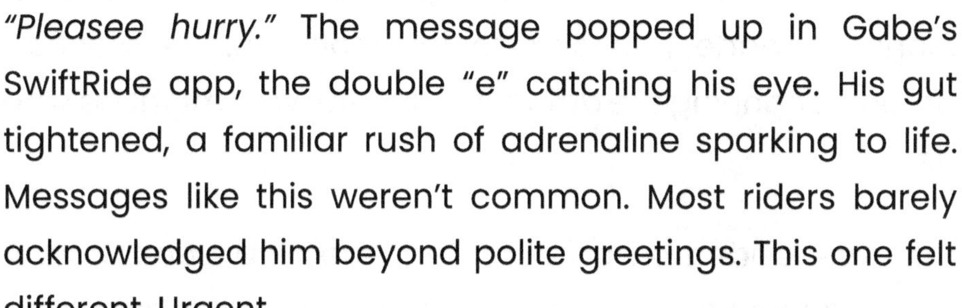

"Pleasee hurry." The message popped up in Gabe's SwiftRide app, the double "e" catching his eye. His gut tightened, a familiar rush of adrenaline sparking to life. Messages like this weren't common. Most riders barely acknowledged him beyond polite greetings. This one felt different. Urgent.

He pressed harder on the gas, ignoring the app's blinking warning about exceeding the speed limit. His focus stayed locked on the destination marker on the screen. One more turn.

As he approached the curb in front of the Epicenter, he spotted her. A woman, swaying unsteadily, one hand grasping at nothing as if searching for an anchor. Her head dipped forward, and her movements were sluggish, disjointed. Gabe's chest tightened. *Something isn't right.*

500 feet. His foot pressed down harder. The engine roared in response, closing the gap in seconds.

She crumpled just as he reached her, collapsing sideways onto the pavement. *No. No. No.* The tires screeched as he slammed the brakes, throwing the car into park and bolting from the driver's seat.

His heart pounded as he knelt beside her, cradling her head in the crook of his arm. Her chestnut waves spilled over his arm, and her skin was pale, clammy. Vulnerable. Alone. It made him sick to his stomach. He glanced around, scanning the atrium for anyone who might be with her.

His eyes landed on a figure near the club's entrance. A man leaned casually against the doorframe, his gaze fixed on them. Watching. The pit in Gabe's stomach deepened. His instincts screamed at him to confront the guy, to demand answers, to figure out what the hell was going on. *One thing at a time.*

He turned his attention back to the woman, forcing his focus to narrow. He checked for a pulse at her neck. It was there, strong and steady. Relief mingled with determination. "Good girl," he murmured, his voice low, almost to himself.

"Hey. Can you hear me?" His voice was firm now, cutting through the chaos in his mind. Nothing. He shook her gently, then harder. Still nothing. Gabe resorted to a sternum rub, the knuckles of his hand grinding into the center of her chest. Not even a flinch.

Someone slipped her something. His jaw tightened as the realization settled in. He carefully lifted her, cradling her limp form as he carried her to the backseat of his car.

As he secured her in the seat, his mind flicked to his case. Six months undercover, driving drunks across the city while trying to untangle the threads of a human trafficking operation. Six months of nothing but secondhand stories, vague leads, and dead ends. Yet the RidgeRunner kept surfacing—its name whispered in reports of women disappearing into the night.

He glanced back at her, a thought slipping through the flood of urgency: *Is she connected to this? To them?*

Shaking off the thought, he climbed into the driver's seat, glancing in the rearview mirror at her motionless figure. His hands gripped the wheel, his knuckles white. *Focus. Get her safe.*

The hospital was only ten minutes away. But to Gabe, it felt like a lifetime.

On a sunny June day, under a cloudless Carolina sky, three women disappeared.

University students Nicole Carter, Amber Resson, and Lindsey Platt had rented a boat for the weekend on Lake Norman. It was the kind of thing anyone would do at the peak of a Carolina summer—laugh, soak in the sun, escape the grind of college life. But by Sunday evening, their phones had gone silent. Friends and family reported the last thing they knew: the girls had been boating. After that, nothing. Three vibrant lives—gone without a trace.

Gabe had read their names so many times they felt like ghosts haunting him. Nicole. Amber. Lindsey. He could see their faces every time he closed his eyes, smiling in the photos that accompanied the case file. Young, full of promise, unaware their carefree weekend would take a dark turn. The horrors he imagined they might have endured were relentless, gnawing at him with every dead-end lead.

During the investigation's early days, police learned the girls had been friendly with another group at the docks. The boat rental clerk—a freckled, shirtless kid with a perpetual sunburn—remembered they'd been chatting and laughing with a few men. But the details were frustratingly vague.

No ID, no credit card—just cash. And the one ID the clerk remembered seeing had turned out to be fake. Of course, it had been fake. That would've been too easy.

At least the kid had overheard part of their conversation. "The RidgeRunner," he'd told detectives. The men had mentioned meeting up at the bar later that night. It wasn't much, but it was all they had for months.

Gabe had combed through the reports, trying to piece together a pattern. Spiked drinks. Assaults. Disappearances. Women waking up in strange places with no memory of how they got there. The connection to the RidgeRunner was circumstantial, but it was enough for the Chief to send someone undercover.

And that someone had been Gabe.

He'd been on thin ice at the precinct—nothing major, just a series of minor missteps that had added up. Maybe it was the Chief's way of giving him a shot at redemption, or maybe it was just an assignment no one else wanted. Either way, Gabe had taken it. Six months of blending into the background, ferrying drunken patrons across town while chasing whispers and shadows. Six months, and he was no closer to finding the missing women.

He rubbed a hand over his face, the memory of their names and faces gnawing at him. Nicole. Amber. Lindsey. They deserved more than empty leads and false hope. *I'll find them. I have to.*

Quickly rounding the car, Gabe slid into the driver's seat and shifted into gear. He made a quick call to the hospital's emergency room—another heads-up about an incoming patient. By now, he could probably ask for a punch card with how often he'd dropped off patrons for alcohol poisoning or worse.

As he maneuvered through the streets, he texted his handler, keeping it short and efficient:

"Pick up tonight: 20-something female, suspect she was roofied, headed to the hospital. Stand by for update."

Gabe's messages were always to the point, stripped of any extraneous detail. Once he saw the double checkmark confirming delivery, he deleted them. *Just in case.* His cover wasn't elaborate—no fancy aliases, no disguises. He didn't need them. People rarely asked a rideshare driver for more than their name, and most didn't bother even with that. But it was amazing what people would say when they thought you were invisible.

He glanced in the rearview mirror, his eyes landing on the woman in the backseat. Still motionless, but her chest rose and fell steadily. *Good. She's breathing.*

The screen lit up with a reply from Jenkins, his handler: *"I'll add it to the file. Stand by for updates. You good?"*

Gabe smirked faintly. Jenkins was solid. Grounded. No fluff, no pretense. Gabe liked to think their partnership worked because they were a good match—a team. But the truth? No one else wanted to work with him after Finn. *Or maybe after how I acted when I lost Finn.*

"Always," he replied simply, dropping the phone onto the passenger seat.

Finn.

Gabe's thoughts drifted to Finley "Finn" Stewart. They'd met at the academy, paired together so often during training that they had no choice but to get along. Their similar size and build made them ideal partners for drills, but it was in the classroom that they truly clicked.

Physical training was grueling, and Gabe's natural tendency to bulldoze through problems sometimes left him tense, his movements sharp and hurried. Finn was his counterbalance—calm, measured, and patient. He had a knack for reminding Gabe that precision could be just as powerful as brute force. *And I made sure he was on time.*

Years later, both had clawed their way onto the SWAT team. The training was grueling, pushing them to limits they hadn't thought possible. Every drill, every exercise, honed their instincts and tested their resilience. Together, they'd tackled scenarios meant to break them, coming out sharper, faster, better.

When Gabe got the call that he'd made the team, it was Finn he celebrated with. They'd made it—together. Best of the best.

And then I let him down.

The thought hit like a gut punch, sudden and sharp. Gabe gripped the steering wheel tighter, his knuckles whitening. Finn wasn't just a partner. He was a brother, forged in the fire of shared trauma, late-night drills, and too many close calls. SWAT had been different—it wasn't about camaraderie over coffee or jokes at the precinct. It was trust, built on knowing the guy next to you would take a bullet for you if it came to it. And Finn had.

The memory was one he tried to shove down but never could. Finn had saved his life that day, and Gabe had been powerless to return the favor.

Gabe's car screeched to a stop at the ambulance bay doors, the glow of the Emergency Room's floodlights bouncing off the windshield. A pair of nurses rushed out with a stretcher, one of them unmistakably Annie. She was always working. Then again, so was he.

"Whatcha got for me tonight?" Annie asked, already pulling on gloves and assessing the unconscious woman as they carefully transferred her to the stretcher. Her tone was casual, almost routine, but her eyes were sharp, scanning every detail.

"Got a message through the app—panicked, sloppy. Found her sitting on the curb outside the RidgeRunner. She passed out just as I arrived," Gabe said, his voice steady despite the churn of frustration beneath the surface.

Annie rolled her eyes dramatically, chewing a piece of gum like it was her coping mechanism for dealing with humanity's stupidity. "The RidgeRunner again. Surprise, surprise."

Her words hit harder than they should have. Gabe forced his expression to remain neutral, but guilt curled in his stomach. *That's my job. To figure that place out. And I've got nothing.* Six months undercover, and every lead felt like smoke slipping through his fingers. Circumstantial evidence, whispers, rumors—nothing concrete enough to act on.

"Yeah," he muttered tightly. "figures."

He followed the stretcher as Annie and her team rolled it into the ER, his focus narrowing on the woman. She looked so small, vulnerable, the vibrant energy she'd likely had earlier in the evening drained away. They stopped in a sterile room devoid of any warmth or personality.

"She seemed kind of panicked when I pulled up," Gabe offered, choosing his words carefully. He couldn't risk revealing too much, not even to Annie, who knew him better than most.

Annie, efficient as always, didn't miss a beat. "You think she was drugged?"

Gabe shrugged, keeping his tone casual. "Could be. Hard to say."

Annie called out to a coworker to order a drug panel as she slipped an IV into place with practiced ease. Gabe watched as the clear fluids began to flow, willing them to do their job.

"I don't know much else," he added, glancing at the monitors as they blinked to life. "But she seemed to be alone. Mind if I stick around to make sure she's okay?"

He wasn't proud of playing the Good Samaritan angle, but it wasn't entirely a lie. Part of him genuinely wanted to make sure she'd pull through. And yeah, she was stunning—even now, with her smudged makeup and tousled hair. There was something striking about her, something that stirred a protective instinct deep in his gut.

But this wasn't just about her beauty. Gabe needed answers. Details. Faces. Names.

Annie rummaged through the small bag slung across the woman's body. Gabe hadn't touched it when he'd picked her up, prioritizing getting her to the hospital as fast as possible. And honestly, rifling through a woman's purse wasn't a great look for anyone—least of all a rideshare driver.

"Isabelle Reed," Annie read aloud, holding up the ID just as the woman's eyes fluttered open at the sound of her name.

For a brief moment, fear exploded across her face. Her blue eyes, stormy and wild, locked onto his, stopping him cold.

"It's okay," Gabe said gently, his voice low and steady despite the rough edge it naturally carried. "I'm your driver, Gabe." He softened his expression, trying to project calm. The last thing he wanted was to scare her more. *I need this. I need her.*

She fought to stay conscious, her eyes darting around the room, but the drug was relentless. Her eyelids fluttered, then closed, as she was pulled under again.

Annie gestured toward a stiff, worn chair in the corner. "Might as well get comfortable," she said, already moving to check Isabelle's vitals.

Gabe ran a hand over the back of his neck as he sank into the chair, its cushion threatening to spill out from a frayed corner. His eyes drifted back to Isabelle, her breathing now steady, though her face remained pale.

Another night. Another hope for a break. Another reminder of what I owe.

He repositioned in the chair, unable to get comfortable. Sleep wouldn't come easy. It never did. Gabe stayed, his mind circling the same unrelenting thoughts: hoping, praying that tonight would give him something—anything—to make his failings, and the penance he owed, matter.

CHAPTER 7

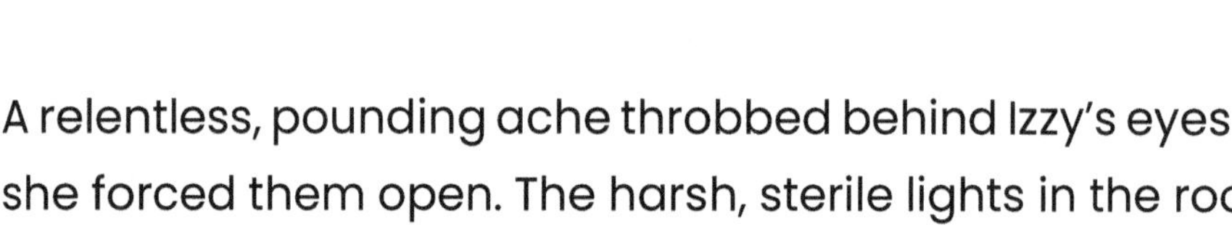

A relentless, pounding ache throbbed behind Izzy's eyes as she forced them open. The harsh, sterile lights in the room assaulted her vision, making her squint against the brightness. Her throat felt like sandpaper, and each breath seemed thick and heavy, clinging to her lungs. She tried to swallow, but her mouth was dry and scratchy, protesting every movement.

Blinking to focus, she caught sight of a figure slumped in a chair in the corner of the room. A man. Recognition hovered just out of reach, teasing the edges of her foggy mind. *Who is that?*

She looked down, noticing the green hospital gown covering her body and the tubes trailing from her arm. The room was a symphony of faint beeps, muffled voices, and hurried footsteps from the hallway beyond the door. She struggled to piece together how she'd ended up here but came up empty. Her focus narrowed to one all-consuming sensation: thirst.

Clearing her throat weakly, she reached for the jug of water on the bedside tray, pulling it toward her with trembling hands. She drank greedily, the cool liquid soothing her parched throat.

The man stirred, his eyes snapping open as he sat upright. Their gazes met awkwardly over the jug, and Izzy froze mid-sip.

"Do you remember me?" His voice was rough with sleep, deep and gravelly.

Izzy squinted, her temples protesting the effort. "You look familiar…" Her voice cracked, thick and unfamiliar to her ears. Clearing her throat, she tried again. "I'm sorry. Everything's… fuzzy."

"Please don't apologize," he said, leaning forward slightly. "I'm Gabe. I was, uh… your ride home last night."

Her brow furrowed. "You were taking me home? From the club?" Heat flushed her cheeks. "That just seems so unlike me. I—" She cut herself off, covering her face with her hands.

"No! No, I'm sorry," Gabe said quickly, his own face tinged with embarrassment. "I was your driver. From SwiftRide. You passed out on the curb outside the RidgeRunner."

Izzy's stomach twisted. Her mind raced, grappling with the humiliation of the situation. *Would it be so bad if he took me home?* The thought was fleeting, she dismissed it quickly. *I'm probably not his type.*

Trying to compose herself, Izzy smoothed her tousled hair. Her cheeks burned hotter as she realized how much of a mess she must look. *Great. Just great.*

"Thank you," she said softly, glancing down at the heavy hospital blankets. "For bringing me here." Her voice faltered. "You stayed? All night?"

Gabe shifted in the uncomfortable-looking chair. "Yeah. I didn't feel right leaving you alone." He rubbed the back of his neck, his words awkward but sincere. "I hope that doesn't make you feel weird. I just..." He hesitated, then added, "I didn't like the idea of you being alone like that."

A strange sensation stirred in Izzy's chest at his kindness— a flutter, unfamiliar and long dormant.

"No, it's…" She trailed off, struggling to articulate her thoughts. "I don't remember much. It feels like… like a piece of my brain is missing."

Gabe nodded, his expression sympathetic. "It must be disorienting. The nurse said your drug screen came back positive for Rohypnol."

The words landed heavily. She'd suspected it, but hearing it confirmed sent a chill through her. Gabe's voice softened. "What's the last thing you remember?"

Izzy tried to dredge up the night's events, her mind wading through the sludge of her fractured memories. Getting ready with Sophie. Arriving at the club. Bits of conversation with the sorority girls. Sophie's laugh, bright and warm at their table. Other moments were fragments, smoke just out of reach.

"I was with Sophie," she said slowly, trying to organize her thoughts.

"Do you think your friends might know more?" Gabe asked.

"They're not my friends," she snapped, then winced at her tone.

Gabe raised an eyebrow, taken aback but patient.

"I'm sorry," Izzy sighed. "I shouldn't have snapped. Sophie's my friend. I can text her. She'll know something."

She pulled out her phone, her fingers fumbling slightly as she typed: **"*Something weird happened last night. Call me ASAP.*"**

"Ah. That's why you were leaving alone, then?" Gabe asked casually, though his eyes were sharper now, focused.

"Yeah. Sophie insisted I go out, but it's not my scene. She'll probably never get me to go again after this." Izzy forced a weak laugh. "Silver linings, right?"

She glanced down at her phone. *Undelivered.* A twinge in her gut sent up a red flag.

Izzy frowned, sending another text to the group chat Sophie had included her in the previous evening: *"Sophie's not answering. Can someone have her call me ASAP?"*

"She didn't meet up with you?" asked a girl in the chat— Gabby, maybe? Izzy couldn't quite place her.

"She left shortly after you did, babe. I think she went home with that guy she was dancing with."

Izzy's blood ran cold. Fragments of memory crashed into her: sandy hair, an expensive watch, that uneasy feeling.

The whiskey and soda.

The realization hit like a punch to the gut. *Sophie drank it.*

Izzy's eyes widened in terror as she looked at Gabe. "I'm gonna be sick."

Gabe acted fast, grabbing a nearby bucket and holding her hair back as she retched violently. His touch was steady, his hand warm and comforting against her back. Izzy clung to the support, breathing raggedly as she tried to collect herself.

When she finally looked up, her voice trembled. "Sophie's missing."

CHAPTER 8

GABRIEL

It hadn't taken much for Gabe to convince Isabelle—Izzy, as she'd quickly asked him to call her—that she should accept his help. He liked the nickname. It suited her. To keep his cover intact, he'd advised her to file an official police report, spinning a story about having "connections" in the city. It wasn't entirely a lie, but it still left a sour taste in his mouth. *This is the part I hate—lying to good people. Even if it's for the right reasons.*

First, though, a pit stop.

Gabe double-checked the number on the door and sighed. *This must be it.* Izzy's panic had reignited earlier that morning when she realized her dog, Marshall, was still at home. *"He must be worried sick!"* she'd exclaimed, guilt heavy in her voice.

The nurse hadn't budged on letting Izzy leave early—something about her electrolytes needing correction—so she was stuck at the hospital for another night. Wanting to earn her trust, Gabe had offered to check on Marshall. He shouldn't have been so quick to volunteer.

"Protective" was the word she kept using to describe him. Protective and 105 pounds. Great.

Gabe pulled out his phone and called Izzy. Her face appeared on the screen, her expression torn between gratitude and worry as she coached him through the process. He unlocked the door gingerly, hearing sniffing under the door frame almost immediately, followed by a low whine.

Pushing the door open, he slid the phone inside first. Izzy's high-pitched, sing-song voice filled the room, and Gabe couldn't help the smirk creeping onto his face as she baby-talked her massive dog. *Marshmallow. Seriously?*

A wide, wet snout pressed against his hand, sniffing him like he was hiding something suspicious. The door creaked open wider as a huge head pushed against it. "It's okay," Gabe said low and steady, as Izzy cooed through the phone, *"Marshmallow, my good boyyy. Be niiiice. He's a friend!"*

The sniffing intensified, and the dog tilted his head at the phone, puzzled. Gabe crouched low, extending a hand cautiously. The dog growled softly, his body tensed, but Izzy's soothing voice cut through his defenses. Slowly, Marshmallow sat, his suspicious gaze fixed on Gabe. After another sniff, the dog harrumphed and turned away as if to say, *Fine, but I don't like it.*

After seeing to the dog's needs, Gabe tried for some affection—a pat on the side—but Marshmallow simply walked off, unimpressed. *So much for bonding.*

Securing the dog inside while he retrieved Izzy's things proved impossible. As Gabe tried to leave, the beast wedged himself between him and the door. "No. You stay," Gabe commanded firmly, attempting to push the dog back inside. Marshmallow slipped through the opening with surprising agility, plopping himself stubbornly on the other side. His tail wagged once, triumphant.

Gabe called Izzy, holding up the phone like a white flag. "He's not letting me leave without him."

Izzy's laughter rang through the line. "It would save gas to take him with you, you know. He's a good snuggler!"

Gabe sighed, his resistance crumbling. "Alright, dude," he muttered, looking at the dog. "But if you pee in my car, you're out."

Later, Gabe waited in his car at the storage facility, the afternoon sun bouncing off the metal doors and casting jagged shadows. It was their designated meeting spot— remote and discreet, with shoddy security footage and no sound recording.

Jenkins pulled up in a plain black sedan, his hazel eyes squinting against the sunlight as he stepped out. His casual attire made him look more like an off-duty coach than an officer, but Gabe knew better.

Jenkins raised an eyebrow at the enormous white dog occupying Gabe's back seat. "Don't ask," Gabe muttered. *Every inch of my car is covered in fur.*

They exchanged a firm handshake before Gabe scanned the area to ensure they were alone. Lowering his voice, he launched into the details of the case, recounting Izzy's drugging, her friend Sophie's disappearance, and the description of the man likely responsible. Jenkins scribbled furiously on a notepad, nodding occasionally as Gabe pieced together the events.

"This is the most we've had to go on so far," Jenkins said, his voice charged with renewed energy. "Good thing your girl got out when she did."

My girl? The phrasing caught Gabe off guard, but he didn't correct him.

"We need someone to follow up at the RidgeRunner," Gabe suggested. "Check the cameras, talk to staff, see if they remember anything."

Jenkins shook his head. "Man, I'd love to. But the Chief wants us lying low. If we go nosing around, we risk spooking them into moving somewhere else."

Gabe ran a hand through his curls, frustration simmering beneath the surface. *They finally had a lead, and now they had to tread lightly?*

"What if Izzy does the asking?" Gabe offered. "She's desperate to find her friend, and it wouldn't raise as many red flags. I could give her some pointers, keep an eye on things in case it goes south."

Jenkins hesitated, but eventually nodded. "Solid plan. Just make sure she's safe. If it gets messy, pull her out."

"Always," Gabe replied, his voice steady.

As Gabe drove away, Marshmallow's tail thumped against the seat, shedding more fur into the air. For the first time in months, Gabe felt a sense of purpose. He wasn't just chasing ghosts anymore. There was a path forward.

For Finn. For Izzy. For Sophie.

And maybe, just maybe, for himself.

CHAPTER 9

It had been twelve hours since Izzy realized Sophie was missing—taken. The initial, visceral dread that had emptied her stomach was now a dull, persistent hum in the background. She wondered if it would become her constant companion. *Is this what grief feels like?*

She was exhausted from recounting the same fragmented memories again and again. It felt like smearing paint onto a canvas in haphazard strokes, hoping the picture would eventually make sense. But Izzy had never had patience for art. She wanted answers, not abstract impressions.

The police arrived about an hour after she'd woken up, summoned once the hospital confirmed her drug test results. Gabe had left before their arrival, promising he'd do whatever he could to help find Sophie. Izzy wasn't sure what possessed him to get involved—it wasn't like they were close. But she couldn't shake the sense that Gabe carried his own demons. Normally, she preferred to handle things alone, but even she knew she was in way over her head this time.

His presence, brief as it had been, had kept her grounded when the situation felt too surreal to handle. For once, it didn't feel like Izzy versus the world. She appreciated that more than she wanted to admit.

The officers had been polite but detached at first, explaining that they typically waited 24 hours before taking missing persons reports seriously. *They usually show up one way or another.* Izzy's stomach twisted at the implications. She mentioned her drug screen results, the signs of foul play, and that seemed to finally shift their approach.

The questions came relentlessly after that, one detail after another, until her head felt like it might split open. By the time the officers left, Izzy's body was still, but her mind was racing. She couldn't just sit there. The urge to act buzzed through her like static, fraying her nerves. Being confined to the hospital bed made it worse. *And I thought I felt helpless on that curb. Give it a day, Izz. Ha.*

One by one, Izzy called the sorority girls from the group thread, her fingers trembling slightly as she scrolled through the names. She asked the same questions over and over: Did anyone see Sophie leave? Did they notice the sandy-haired man? Did anything stand out?

Most of the responses were polite but unhelpful, apologies wrapped in useless details that confirmed what Izzy already knew. By the time she reached the last name on the list, frustration had burned away her exhaustion, leaving a hot coil of anger in its place.

How could they let this happen? Izzy thought bitterly. These so-called friends went out with Sophie all the time and didn't notice when something was wrong? Didn't fight for her?

When Gabby, the brunette, answered, her voice cracked with emotion. She rambled through a cacophony of memories, recounting Sophie's bright personality as if she were already gone.

She's not dead! Izzy wanted to scream. *She can't be.*

The thought sent her spiraling into memories of Sophie—the lanky, awkward middle schooler who had been Izzy's rock before either of them had grown into themselves. Sophie hadn't been the beauty she'd later become, but even then, her warmth was undeniable. She overflowed with kindness and an infectious laugh that could light up the darkest day.

Sophie had always seen the good in people, even when it wasn't obvious. It was something Izzy had secretly envied. Where Izzy was guarded, skeptical, Sophie was open and endlessly giving. But Sophie wasn't naive. When it came to protecting the people she loved, she was a fortress—unyielding and fierce.

Izzy's mind wandered to a middle school hallway, where a group of mean girls had been gossiping loudly about "brace face Isabelle." Izzy had been ready to endure the humiliation in silence, slipping away to avoid them. But Sophie had been having none of it.

Sweet, loyal Sophie had marched straight up to the bullies, her voice sharp and clear as she told them exactly how beautiful, capable, and brilliant her best friend was. Then, with a perfectly straight face, Sophie had threatened to sneak into their rooms at night and hide slimy, warty toads in their bedsheets if they ever insulted Izzy again.

Izzy couldn't help but smile at the memory, the vivid image of Sophie's satisfied smirk as she turned on her heel and left the girls slack-jawed. *They never bothered me again.*

The ache in Izzy's chest grew sharper as she thought about Sophie, picturing her as that fierce, fearless girl who'd always fought for her friends. *I'll fight for you now, Soph. Wherever you are, I'll find you.*

Izzy dialed the number for Madison, the blonde from the group. Her fingers tightened around the phone as it rang. *Please, give me something.*

Madison answered almost immediately, her voice already thick with emotion. Of course, she already knew Sophie was missing. Izzy could picture the sorority house in chaos, the girls pacing and crying, feeding off each other's dramatics. The thought made Izzy's stomach churn. *Where was this energy when Sophie didn't come home?*

Madison's voice wavered, repeating over and over how worried she was. Izzy clenched her teeth, swallowing the urge to snap at her. *Save the sob story and help me find my friend.* Instead, she waited for the blubbering to subside.

"Madison," Izzy said, her tone firm but calm, "I really need to know if you noticed anything weird or different that night. Literally, anything you can recall might be helpful. My memory's still a little fuzzy…"

Madison sniffled audibly. "I don't know. I remember that guy bringing you a drink. He seemed, like, hot enough—not sleazy or anything…"

Izzy rolled her eyes, forcing herself to focus. She grabbed the hospital stationery the nurse had left behind and jotted down Madison's words. *Hot enough? Seriously?*

Madison continued rambling. "But, um, it did seem weird how often he was talking to the bartender. Like, you'd think he'd have been there with a buddy or something."

Izzy's pen froze mid-scribble. "Wait. What'd you say?" Her heartbeat quickened, her exhaustion momentarily forgotten.

Madison's voice faltered. "Uh, just… it seemed odd. He kept going back to the bartender before he came over to the table."

The words sparked a memory—brief, but vivid. Izzy and Sophie arriving at the RidgeRunner. The sandy-haired man had been at the bar then, talking to the bartender before turning to look at them.

Izzy's pulse raced. "Thanks for your help, Madison. I'll let you know if we come up with anything." She ended the call abruptly, not waiting for Madison's reply.

Her fingers hovered over the screen for a moment before dialing Gabe's number. Adrenaline surged through her, mingling with a fragile hope. *This has to mean something. Please, let this mean something.*

"Hey," she said the moment he picked up. "I think I've got something."

CHAPTER 10

GABRIEL

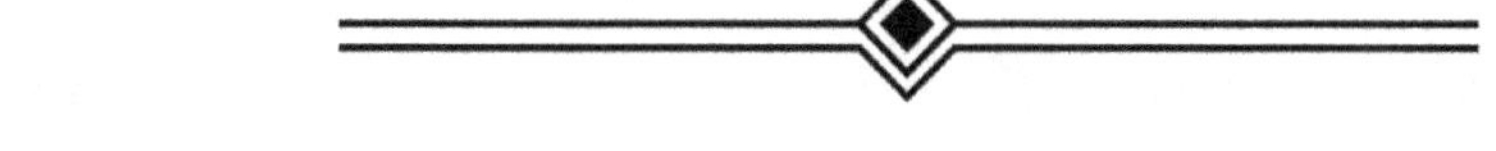

Sweat beads on my forehead as we prepare to breach the front door. My heart thunders in my chest—a war drum beating a rhythm to steady my mind. *Point man: first in, last out.*

The signal alerts me. It's time.

The door shatters under the battering ram's force, wood splintering into a cascade of sharp fragments. Darkness rushes to meet me, heavy and suffocating. My breathing steadies, falling into a practiced cadence.

In, two, three, four. Out, two, three, four.

The light from my rifle's mount cuts through the black as I sweep the room, inch by inch. Shadows creep along the walls, shifting as the beam dances across the cluttered space. My senses are sharp, every sound amplified, every corner a potential threat.

Finn's hand grips the back of my vest, grounding me. He's always there—my six, my brother. I press forward, my voice cutting through the oppressive silence as I clear each section. *Steady. Keep moving. Find the threat.*

The living room is a wreck, furniture overturned, and debris scattered. The smell of fear and adrenaline—mine and my team's—hangs in the air. My pulse hammers as I scan the room, muscles coiled, ready for the fight I know is coming.

And then I see it.

A demon, black as midnight, slithering from the shadows, its grin grotesque, its teeth a stark, predatory white. My body tenses, every instinct screaming at me to move, to react. But my feet are rooted to the ground, as if the darkness itself holds me captive.

Move! My mind roars, but my body won't obey.

The demon lunges, its form blurring as it leaps toward me. A shot rings out, sharp and deafening, shattering the silence.

I turn, my voice a desperate plea. *Take me instead. Please. Take me.*

The grip on my vest falls slack.

Gabe jolted awake, his body drenched in sweat, his breath coming in ragged gasps. The weight of the dream lingered, pressing heavily on his chest. *Another nightmare. Another failure brought to life.*

He wiped a hand over his face, forcing himself to focus on the room around him. It was a routine he'd perfected, a way to pull himself out of the past and back into reality.

The small nightstand beside his bed held his phone, wallet, and keys, strewn in their usual chaos. A modest dresser stood against the wall, barren except for a single photo in a simple frame. It was the only one he owned—him and Finn, arms slung around each other, grinning amidst a group of friends on the day they made SWAT. Finn's smile was wide and unrestrained, while Gabe's was more subdued, reflecting his serious nature.

You brought out the best in me, buddy.

Across the room, the mirrored doors of the closet reflected his image back at him. Dark circles shadowed his eyes, his face pale and drawn. He rubbed his temples, willing away the lingering unease.

At the foot of the bed, Marshall lay curled in a tight ball, his massive frame improbably compact. The blanket Gabe had left on the floor for him had clearly been ignored.

"Figures," Gabe muttered, shaking his head. The dog cracked one eye open at the sound of his voice before resettling.

His thoughts drifted to Izzy, to her soft chestnut waves and piercing blue eyes. Something about her had a way of quieting the storm inside him, even if only for a moment.

Throwing back the covers, Gabe swung his legs over the side of the bed and grabbed his phone. A message from Izzy caught his eye—an update about her discharge. They'd planned for him to pick her up later that day.

He snapped a quick photo of Marshall sprawled on the bed, his massive paws splayed across the covers.

"Your dog is spoiled," he texted, smirking as he hit send.

Her reply came quickly, filled with endearments for the dog and completely ignoring his comment. Gabe chuckled softly, the corner of his mouth lifting. She was eager to track down her lead, her determination radiating even through the screen.

So am I, Izzy, Gabe thought, the faint smile fading as his focus shifted. He wasn't just chasing shadows anymore. This lead might finally take them one step closer to answers—for Sophie, for Izzy, and for himself.

During Izzy's time in the hospital, conversation became the default way to fill the hours. She told Gabe about her life—her friendship with Sophie, her dad back home, and her relentless pursuit of investigative journalism, which had landed her a residency at a media company. Her voice lit up when she spoke about her ambitions, but there was an undercurrent of pain when she mentioned her ex-boyfriend and the suspicious car accident that had supposedly claimed his life.

Gabe's mind sharpened at that detail. He remembered the reports of the accident. No body recovered. There was more to the story—he could feel it—but Izzy held back, her tone tightening whenever Liam came up. Her body language was enough to tell Gabe the guy had been a jerk. He didn't press her, but he filed the information away.

Izzy was perceptive and refreshingly sharp, with a knack for digging into details. Yet, what stood out most was how deeply she seemed to care—about Sophie, her dad, her work. Gabe found himself drawn to her sincerity, a quality that felt rare in his world of half-truths and ulterior motives.

When Izzy asked about his history, Gabe stuck to the script: raised in a house full of brothers, always trying to prove himself. It was enough to satisfy her curiosity without diving into the messy details he either had to hide or lie about. He hated this part of his job—building connections while knowing he could never fully be himself.

But something about Izzy made him want to break that rule.

"I, uh, lost someone recently, too," Gabe said, his voice rough as he cleared his throat. He hadn't meant to say it, hadn't planned on opening that door, but the words slipped out anyway.

Izzy's brow furrowed, her features softening with quiet sadness. Her blue eyes shimmered, not with pity but with something far more rare: understanding. She didn't try to fix him or offer platitudes. Instead, her voice was a gentle whisper, grounding him. "I'm so sorry."

She placed her hand on his, the gesture simple yet deeply human. Her thumb brushed lightly over his knuckles, and Gabe felt a strange calm settle over him.

"He was like a brother to me," Gabe said, his voice low, barely above a whisper. The weight of the memory pressed against him, but he kept going, carefully choosing his words. "He died last year. Suddenly."

The final word was clipped, raw with emotion. He prayed she wouldn't ask for more details—didn't want to lie to her, but couldn't afford the truth.

"Ever since, I've felt... stuck," he admitted, his voice dropping further. "Like I can't change it. Can't help anyone." The honesty startled him, the words slipping past his defenses before he could stop them. "Every day feels like I'm trapped, reliving the same moments."

What he didn't say hung heavy in the air between them: *And I'm still here, living without him.*

Izzy surprised him. She didn't recoil from his grief or fill the silence with empty reassurances. Instead, she leaned in, offering something far more profound: empathy. Her presence was steady, unflinching, as if she were quietly pulling him back from the edge.

In that moment, when he'd intended to comfort her, she had reached across the space between them, anchoring him instead.

It was strange—the gentleness she offered, the quiet strength that softened the heaviness of his words. Yet even in her kindness, Gabe could see the fortress she'd built around herself, the walls forged from years of solitude. He knew that fortress well; it mirrored his own.

But Izzy's loneliness felt different. It wasn't born of bitterness or resentment. It was the kind that came from giving too much, from pouring herself out for others without ever learning how to protect herself in return.

Gabe felt the shift between them then. It wasn't dramatic or loud, but something clicked into place—a silent understanding, a shared recognition. Neither of them was truly alone anymore, not in this moment.

For the first time in a long time, Gabe wondered if that could be enough.

IZZY

Getting into Gabe's car outside the hospital felt strange. Stranger still was asking him to rummage through her closet to bring her clothes. The memory of explaining which drawer held her underthings still burned in her mind. *I know. I know. I could've called my dad.* But the idea was unthinkable. He'd been hovering for months, treating her like a fragile doll after everything that had happened. *If I told him I stubbed my toe, he'd probably bubble-wrap me.*

Gabe had been surprisingly gracious about it all, though Izzy got the distinct impression he wasn't exactly a dog person. *It probably seems insane to trust a virtual stranger to dig through my apartment, let alone my lingerie drawer. But after what happened at the bar... maybe trusting my gut isn't such a bad idea.*

Trust wasn't something Izzy gave easily, but Gabe was different. He was straightforward—maybe a little too blunt at times—but she appreciated his lack of pretense. She'd had her fill of smooth-talking liars who danced around the truth.

And after everything she'd been through—lying on a curb, unconscious, defenseless, puking in a bucket, and blubbering about her dog—there wasn't much more vulnerable she could be in front of a man. *Okay, the underwear was a new low.* Yet even now, she couldn't figure out what he stood to gain by helping her. A part of her wanted to believe he was just... kind. *Could people really help simply because they cared?*

Outside the car, Izzy squished Marshmallow's enormous face, her fingers buried in his plush fur. White clouds of stray hair puffed into the midday air as she scratched his ears, the dog leaning into her touch. She tilted her face toward the sun, letting its warmth chase away the cold ache that had settled in her chest over the past few days. She whispered a silent prayer for Sophie, her lips barely moving.

When she opened her eyes, Gabe was watching her, his gaze curious and sharp.

"What?" she asked, a playful edge in her voice as her cheeks warmed under his scrutiny.

He smirked and shook his head as he opened the driver's side door. "Nothin'," he replied, his grin lingering.

Izzy ignored him, taking the opportunity to adjust her waistband before climbing into the car. *I should've told him to grab the comfy ones.* At least the rest of the outfit—a loose pair of jeans, an oversized band tee, and sneakers—was practical. She glanced at him sideways. *Am I that predictable?*

The night before, she'd called him in a frenzy, ready to march into the RidgeRunner in a hospital gown if it meant doing something. He'd calmly suggested she rest first, pointing out that her dress had been taken as evidence, and she'd be underdressed for the occasion.

"Go ahead," he'd teased. "I'll even drive."

Her cheeks had burned at the implication, and her frustration simmered to a slow boil. "Too bad," he'd muttered, his eyes glinting with amusement. "Would've liked to see that."

She'd rolled her eyes, trying to ignore the heat crawling up her neck when he'd called her blush "cute." It took two hours of cajoling and threats before he'd stopped calling her "sweet cheeks."

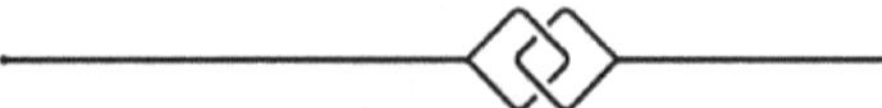

After dropping Marshall off at her apartment with an abundance of reassurances and head scratches, they arrived at the RidgeRunner.

The sight of the bar made Izzy's stomach churn. Memories from that night clawed their way to the surface—flashes of fear, helplessness, and the looming sense of something horribly wrong. She clenched her fists, willing herself to focus. In the daylight, the bar looked harmless, even inviting. But the shadows it cast over her mind wouldn't dissipate so easily.

Breathe. In. Out.

Gabe's hand rested gently on her forearm, his rough palm grounding her. "You need a minute?" he asked softly, his voice low and steady.

His tone wasn't pitying, nor was it impatient. For once, someone wasn't asking if she was okay—they already knew she wasn't. It was a small kindness, but it settled her.

She sighed deeply, tucking stray strands of hair behind her ears. "Yeah. Just a second..."

Her voice wobbled as she admitted, "I hate to think of what's happening to Sophie right now. I feel so helpless—like all this isn't enough. I can't just... wait for news." Her eyes stung, the unfallen tears blurring her view of the atrium. She turned her head, blinking quickly to keep them at bay.

Gabe's hand stayed on her arm, a quiet reassurance that he wasn't going anywhere.

He broke the silence, his voice heavy with a knowing sadness. "I'm not one for false hope, Izz. I can't promise you how this will turn out. But you do what you can, with the time you have." He exhaled, his hand retreating as he gestured toward the RidgeRunner's doors. "This is something we can do. It's not much, but it's a start. And it's better than nothing."

Izzy studied his face, his lips pressed into a thin line, his eyes shadowed by some unspoken grief. Whatever he'd been through, she realized, was driving him now, just as her loss was driving her.

She nodded, letting out a shaky breath as her resolve hardened. She wouldn't let Sophie slip away—not like everything else.

"I'm ready."

She wasn't ready. Not even close. But Gabe followed her through the RidgeRunner's doors, his steady presence like an anchor, and somehow her feet kept moving. Her heart pounded in her chest, a frantic drum beat that matched the wild swirl of her thoughts. She resisted the urge to push Gabe ahead of her, scanning the vast, eerily still room.

The bar and tables sat under the glare of daylight, a stark contrast to the chaos she remembered—or tried not to remember. Gone were the pounding music, the suffocating crowds, the strobing lights that had made everything feel disorienting. *It feels wrong. All of it.*

Knocking lightly, she stepped inside, introducing herself to the middle-aged man hunched over a desk drowning in paper stacks, pen holders, and empty coffee cups. Every chair and surface was buried under chaos, leaving no room for them to sit. *Not one for organization, then.*

Thankfully, her earlier phone call had done most of the explaining. The manager wasted no time leading them to the security room—or rather, a glorified closet crammed with monitors and hard drives. The air felt stale, and the walls pressed in on her, amplifying the thudding of her heart. She wrapped her arms around herself, a futile attempt to shield against the rising tide of emotions threatening to break through.

"You mentioned cameras at the entrances," she said, her voice steady despite the storm building within. "Can we see the footage from that night?"

The manager nodded, scrolling through hours of video. The screens flickered with image after image, bodies moving in and out of the club's doors. Izzy leaned forward, her breath shallow, every fiber of her being focused on the grainy footage.

"Stop!" she blurted suddenly, her finger darting toward the screen. The manager rewound the video, and there she was—Izzy, walking out of the RidgeRunner. Her shoulders sagged with relief in the recording, a moment that felt entirely foreign as she watched herself move.

I don't remember any of this.

"Keep going," she urged. The man advanced the footage, and her breath caught when Sophie appeared on the screen.

"There," she whispered, her voice trembling under the weight of realization. Sophie's beautiful blonde hair caught the light, but her expression was distant, her eyes vacant. *She doesn't even look like herself.*

Izzy's stomach twisted as she spotted the sandy-haired man beside Sophie. His hand gripped her upper arm—not harshly, but firmly enough to make Izzy's blood boil. To a passerby, he might have seemed like a concerned friend helping someone to a car. But Izzy saw the truth in his predatory smile and the unnatural way Sophie stumbled, catching her heel on the door jamb.

"Deceitful monster," Izzy muttered, her voice laced with venom.

Her breath quickened as she studied the scene, her eyes darting across the screen for clues. She barely registered Gabe's hand resting on her back until she turned to meet his gaze. His expression mirrored hers: grave, focused, furious.

"What did the police say about this? Do they know who he is? Are they tracking him down?" The questions tumbled out, panic threading through her words.

The manager blinked, looking confused. "This is the first time we've reviewed it, ma'am."

Her stomach dropped. "You mean to tell me the police haven't been here?"

The man raised his hands defensively. "There's another manager… maybe they talked to him. I don't know. But this footage hasn't been reviewed before."

Izzy's fury was ice-cold, sharp, and focused. She turned to Gabe, her mind spinning with disbelief. *What if no one's been looking for her this whole time? While I was lying in a hospital bed?*

"You know what?" she said, her voice flat and controlled. "Forget it. I need a copy of this footage. Now."

She handed the man a thumb drive from her pocket, and he scrambled to comply.

"And the bartender from that night," she added, her tone brooking no argument. "Where is he?"

The manager stammered, "Uh… Brandon's in the back, on stock duty."

"Great," she said, her posture straightening as she prepared to follow him. "We'll come with you."

The manager hesitated but quickly relented, leading them through narrow hallways that reeked of cleaning supplies and stale beer. Despite her earlier nerves, Izzy felt the cold edge of determination settle over her, sharpening her senses. She glanced back at Gabe, his silent presence reassuring.

When they emerged into a poorly lit alley, Izzy immediately spotted the bartender crouched over a pile of cardboard, cutting up boxes. The moment their eyes met, recognition flared in his expression.

The manager opened his mouth to speak, but Brandon bolted.

Before Izzy could shout, Gabe was already moving. He surged forward with startling speed, weaving through the alley as Brandon threw debris in his path. Izzy didn't hesitate, sprinting after them, her lungs burning as she pushed herself to keep up.

Sophie, I'm coming for you.

Izzy found them at the end of the narrow maze of alleyways, her chest heaving with exertion and adrenaline.

Brandon's face was pressed against a brick wall, his left eye already swelling into what promised to be an ugly bruise. Gabe stood behind him, one arm twisted and pinned at an angle that made Izzy wince just looking at it. Gabe's voice was low and venomous, a steady whisper of anger threading through his clenched teeth.

She paused for a moment, caught off guard by the sheer force of Gabe's presence, before stepping closer.

"Tell her what you told me," Gabe growled, shoving Brandon harder against the wall. The scrape of flesh against brick made the man whimper, his defiance crumbling.

"I don't really know anything, dude!" Brandon yelped.

Gabe applied more pressure, his knuckles whitening. "Try again."

"AGH! Okay! Okay!" Brandon stammered, his voice rising in panic. "I don't know him. He just… he paid me to not look too closely when he bought drinks for certain girls and left with them. That's it! I didn't ask questions."

"Not good enough," Gabe said coldly, his grip tightening.

"Alright, alright!" Brandon's words tumbled out in a rush. "He'd always talk about going to the lake. He drove this slick black car—fancy as hell. That's all I know! I swear!"

Izzy stepped closer, her voice sharp and cutting. "Where is she? The blonde from the other night. Where did he take her?"

Brandon sneered at her, his lip curling in a grotesque snarl. "Are you deaf or just stupid, lady? I already said, I don't know!"

The glob of spit landed on her shoe before she registered what he'd done. Something inside her snapped, a brittle branch cracking under the weight of everything she'd held back. Grief, anger, fear—it all poured out in a relentless wave.

Before she could think, her hand shot out, grabbing his shoulder as she drove her knee into his groin with all the force her body could muster. Brandon's pained howl echoed in the alleyway, and Gabe barely kept him upright as his legs buckled beneath him.

Izzy moved to strike him again, her vision tinged with red, her hands shaking with the urge to cause him pain. *He hurt Sophie. He helped her disappear. What if we never find her?*

Gabe's hand shot up, a barrier between her and Brandon. "Whoa, Izz," he said, his tone firm but calm. "Enough."

Her breaths came ragged and fast, her chest rising and falling with the effort to rein herself in. Her hands clawed through her hair as her thoughts spiraled into chaos. *Breathe. In. Out.* But the fury wouldn't leave her.

A scream ripped from her chest—raw, feral, and full of everything she couldn't put into words. It echoed through the alley, a sound that made even Brandon cower despite his agony.

"You didn't do anything?" Her voice shook, her anger cold now, sharp and precise. "No. You didn't. It's people like you—cowards—who make it so easy for monsters like him to exist."

A sob caught in her throat, choking her words as she crouched low to meet his terrified gaze. Her voice dropped to a whisper, the venom in her tone freezing him in place.

"I hope you rot," she said, her words deliberate and heavy. "I hope the demons you've made your bed with come for you in the night. And when you writhe and scream for mercy, I hope everyone who could've helped turns their back. Just like you did."

Brandon's wide, tear-filled eyes were answer enough. He whimpered, shrinking away from her as she straightened and stepped back.

Gabe watched her carefully, his body tense but his expression unreadable. For a moment, neither of them moved, the weight of her words hanging thick in the air. Then, with a deep breath, Izzy turned and walked away, her fists still clenched at her sides.

Brandon's head disappeared behind the tinted windows of the police car as Izzy watched from the sidewalk. Her arms crossed tightly over her chest, a futile attempt to contain the swirling frustration in her gut. She answered the officer's questions, biting back the urge to unleash her fury about how a young woman had done their investigative work for them. *Catch flies with honey, Izzy.*

The officer offered a tired explanation about "ongoing leads" and "connections that couldn't be discussed at this time." The vague reassurance felt like a slap. *Whatever that means.*

As the car pulled away, Izzy turned to find Gabe leaning against the edge of the alley, his arms crossed. His dark gaze followed her as she approached. Shaking off her frustration, she teased, "Pretty slick moves back there, parkour. Planning on telling me you moonlight as a superhero anytime soon?" A faint smile played on her lips, though it didn't reach her eyes.

Gabe didn't smile back. Instead, he replied matter-of-factly, "No moonlighting. We needed answers, and I made sure we got them."

Izzy raised a brow, half-amused at his bluntness, before glancing over her shoulder at the receding police car. The hollow feeling in her chest deepened. They'd gotten a confession of sorts, but no names, no clear direction. Just scraps. "I think it's bull that they didn't check here first," she muttered, her tone edged with bitterness. "There's something they're not telling us. Don't you think?"

Gabe's lips pressed into a tight line, his posture stiff. He kicked at a loose pebble on the pavement, his eyes fixed on the ground. "Maybe," he said finally. "Could be they're working an angle we don't know about." His voice lacked conviction, and he didn't meet her gaze until the end.

Izzy's intuition sparked. Something was off. Gabe's reaction didn't sit right, but she dismissed it, chalking it up to adrenaline or exhaustion. *Stop reading into everything, Izzy.*

"Yeah, I guess," she murmured, though her doubts lingered. A heavy silence settled between them as the weight of the day pressed down on her. Her thoughts spiraled—dark images of what Sophie might be enduring clawed at her mind. Her stomach churned, and she covered her eyes with her hands, willing the images away. *Breathe. In. Out. Think of Sophie smiling. Think of our hikes, our movie nights.*

Clearing her throat, she turned to Gabe, her voice thick with emotion. "I know this might sound strange, but when Sophie…" Her voice cracked, and she paused, swallowing hard before continuing. "…when one of us had a bad day, we'd eat ice cream and watch movies in our pajamas." Her cheeks flushed at the memory, and she glanced up at Gabe, half-expecting him to laugh.

Instead, his expression softened, his dark eyes searching hers.

"I mean…" she hesitated, biting her lip. "That's what tonight feels like it calls for. And I don't want to be alone." She looked away, her voice barely above a whisper. "So… do you like ice cream?"

For a moment, Gabe just stared at her, and she braced herself for rejection. But then his lips quirked into a sad, understanding smile. His brown eyes shone with warmth, threatening to melt her into a puddle. He came so close that she could feel the heat from his breath as she looked up at him. Her heart thundered as he stood in her space.

A look of amusement spread slowly across his face, and he said, "I could demolish some Rocky Road right now," he said, his voice warm. He reached for his keys, adding, "I'm not sharing with Marshall, though."

Relief washed over her, loosening the knot in her chest. She smiled genuinely, a rare feeling these days. "Deal. Marshall prefers pistachio anyway."

Their ice cream long gone, they lounged on the couch in Izzy's apartment, the warm glow of the autumn sun filtering through the bay window. The fading light painted golden streams across the room, casting shadows that danced softly on the walls. They sat close enough to feel each other's warmth as *Dirty Dancing* played on the screen.

Izzy had insisted Gabe watch the classic film after enduring his action-packed B-movie disaster—an explosion-filled debacle that had made her roll her eyes more times than she could count. To her horror, Gabe had admitted he'd never seen *Dirty Dancing*, which she declared was a travesty in need of immediate remedy.

Minus the occasional comment about Patrick Swayze being the ultimate "man's man" or judgment about a particular dance move, they mostly watched in companionable silence.

Marshall had wedged himself into a perfectly oversized ball against Izzy, his thick fur rising and falling rhythmically as he dozed. Her hand grazed his fur absently, the mindless motion soothing her frayed nerves. But when she reached to rub Marshall's ears, her fingers brushed Gabe's hand.

His hand was rough, calloused—a stark contrast to her own. The accidental touch sent a jolt of electricity straight through her. She jerked her hand back as if burned, her cheeks heating instantly. "Sorry," she mumbled, her voice barely above a whisper.

Gabe's eyes weren't apologetic. They weren't embarrassed either. Instead, they bore into hers with a fiery intensity that stole her breath, holding something she couldn't quite decipher. Amusement? Curiosity? Something more? Her heart thudded against her ribs as her mind raced. *He probably thinks I'm ridiculous. Inviting a man over for ice cream and movies? Maybe he feels bad for me.*

But beneath her spiraling thoughts, a different awareness simmered. The air felt thick—charged, like the moment before a summer storm. *Am I imagining this? Or does he feel it too?*

She stole a glance, but it was a mistake. Gabe lounged against the couch with an effortless confidence, his dark eyes fixed on the screen. Yet even in his relaxed posture, he radiated something magnetic. One arm rested above his head, exposing the lean muscles in his forearm, and his leg stretched out, the other bent casually. It was a picture of quiet strength, but the weight in his gaze hinted at something deeper, something heavier.

Izzy bit her lip and looked away, scolding herself. *Pull it together, Izz. He's just a guy helping you. You're being ridiculous.*

The movie ended, and Gabe stood, stretching. "Thanks for the ice cream," he said, a small grin tugging at the corner of his mouth.

Izzy followed him to the door, her chest tight with a longing she didn't fully understand. She wanted to thank him for more than the company—for his steady presence, for being there when she needed someone most. But the words felt too heavy to say out loud.

"Goodnight, Izz," he said softly, his voice gravelly. His breaths were ragged as he leaned against the door frame, towering over her. For a moment, it seemed as though he might lean closer, his dark eyes dipping to her lips before meeting her gaze again. Her breath hitched, anticipation crackling in the space between them.

But then he blinked, stepped back, and shoved his hands deep into his pockets. With a small nod, he turned and headed down the stairs, his figure disappearing into the twilight.

Izzy closed the door and leaned her forehead against it, exhaling shakily. Alone again, her thoughts took off like a runaway train. *Gabe looked at me differently tonight—didn't he? Or am I imagining it?*

Guilt followed swiftly, washing over her in a cold wave. *The only reason I even know him is because Sophie is in danger. And here I am dissecting his every look. Pathetic.*

Her thoughts shifted, unbidden, to Sophie. The video footage from the bar replayed in her mind—Sophie's lifeless expression, the sandy-haired man's hand on her arm, his predatory grin. Izzy clenched her fists against the door, anger surging through her. *How can someone look the other way? How could the bartender justify doing nothing?*

The memory of Brandon's smug words clawed at her mind. She saw Gabe pinning him to the wall with an ease that was as impressive as it was terrifying. *How did he move so fast?*

Her anger coiled tightly, a visceral force threatening to consume her. But beneath it lay something colder, sharper—fear. They had no answers, no direction. *We're no closer to finding Sophie. Where do we look next? Where are you, Sophie?*

Izzy's throat tightened, and she pressed her forehead harder against the door, as though she could force the storm of emotions to stop. But it didn't. All she could do was breathe. *In. Out. Just keep moving.*

CHAPTER 11

SOPHIE

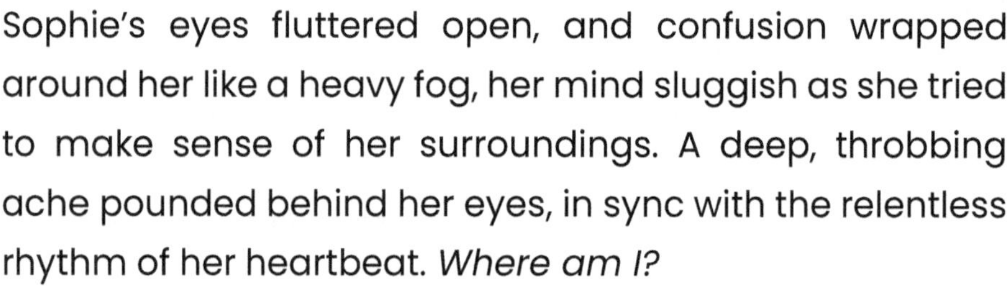

Sophie's eyes fluttered open, and confusion wrapped around her like a heavy fog, her mind sluggish as she tried to make sense of her surroundings. A deep, throbbing ache pounded behind her eyes, in sync with the relentless rhythm of her heartbeat. *Where am I?*

Her breaths quickened, shallow and uneven, as she strained to process her situation. A wave of terror crashed over her as the truth clawed its way to the surface. *I've been taken.*

The darkness was absolute, a rough fabric pressed tightly against her face, blocking all light. Her wrists were bound behind her, the coarse material biting into her skin, making her fingers tingle painfully. She twisted her hands experimentally, her movements sluggish from the lack of blood flow. The faint, damp smell of mold mixed with sweat and something sour invaded her nostrils, making her stomach churn. The nauseating realization struck her: part of the stench could be her. Her bladder screamed for relief, her body betraying her with its urgent, uncomfortable demands. *How long have I been here?*

A sudden lurch of the vehicle sent her skidding across the hard, uneven floor. Her head slammed against something sharp—a bolt, maybe—and pain exploded at the point of contact. She let out a muffled whimper, tears springing to her eyes as blood trickled warmly down her scalp. Her whole body tensed, her breaths coming in short, panicked bursts.

"She's up," a rough, gravelly voice announced. The sound was distant but carried a chill that settled in her chest like ice.

Shuffling footsteps followed, the noise growing louder, closer. Sophie's whimper turned into a desperate sob as the fear of what was coming overwhelmed her. Then the voice was right next to her.

"Shut up," he barked, his tone harsh and commanding. A hand roughly roamed across her body, lingering too long in places that made her skin crawl. She recoiled violently, a strangled cry escaping her throat. *Don't touch me! Don't you dare touch me!*

"Please!" she gasped, her voice cracking from disuse. The words spilled out, desperate and trembling. "I... I need the bathroom. Please. It hurts."

Her sobs punctuated each sentence, and she inhaled deeply, trying to steady herself. But her panic was unrelenting—a tangle of anger, disgust, and sheer terror. Each emotion coiled tightly within her, threatening to suffocate her.

For what felt like an eternity, there was no response. The silence buzzed in her ears, oppressive and heavy. Then, finally:

"Yeah, fine," the man muttered, his voice slick with irritation. He pounded a fist against the side of the vehicle. "Ey! Pull over before she pisses all over the van."

A van. Relief mingled with a renewed surge of fear. She cataloged the detail, her sluggish brain struggling to piece together anything useful. *Who are they? Where are they taking me?*

She inhaled sharply, forcing her spiraling thoughts to slow. She needed to focus, to think clearly. But her mind was a storm, a whirlwind of scattered fragments and questions without answers. *How did I get here?*

What do they say to do when you're kidnapped? The advice she'd heard in passing felt maddeningly distant. She tried to recall anything useful. Counting turns? *Too late for that.* Listening for identifying details? *Nothing stood out about their voices or words.*

Her fingers throbbed painfully as she flexed them against the restraints. She winced, twisting her wrists in tiny, careful movements to ease the ache. Her options felt maddeningly limited.

And then, an idea sparked. It was a flicker of hope, faint but insistent. *It's not much, but it's something.*

The van slowed, its brakes squealing in protest as Sophie braced herself against the jarring stop. She focused intently, straining to decipher every movement, every sound. The vehicle leaned into a curve. *An exit ramp?* She quieted her mind against the pounding in her head, desperate for any clue. A left turn. A straight path for a few minutes. Another left—or a sharp curve? *Damn it.* The roads blurred together in her mind, her disoriented senses offering no clear answer. Bound and blindfolded, she could only piece together fragments, and the realization clawed at her resolve.

She shifted her attention to her hands, her nails. The thick acrylics she'd once admired as pristine were now a lifeline. Wincing, she began working them loose, one by one, the sharp pain biting into her nail beds. Her breaths came shallow and fast as each tug sent a fresh jolt of agony. *Maybe the DNA will help them find my body.* The thought slipped in unbidden, chilling her to her core. *No. I'm not giving up. This has to work. Someone has to find me.*

The van jerked to a halt, tires screeching, and the tension in the air grew palpable. Voices muttered outside, muffled but agitated. Then the door slammed open, and rough hands grabbed her, dragging her out like a sack of grain. Her bare knees scraped against the van's threshold before her feet finally met the ground. She gasped at the cool air, the faint scent of water carried on the breeze. *Water.* She could hear it too, lapping softly against a shore. No crashing waves. *A lake. Lake Norman?*

Her hope surged, fleeting and fragile, only to be crushed by a sharp blow to her ribs. Pain exploded in her side, stealing her breath and doubling her over. "Move," a gruff voice barked, the edge of panic betraying his nerves.

"I—" Sophie gasped, clutching her side as she stumbled forward, her heels catching on uneven ground.

"Could I... please—my hands?" she rasped, her voice hoarse. "It'll take longer if they're tied."

One of them cursed under his breath, and she felt the cold bite of metal against her wrists. Relief flooded her as the restraints snapped free, blood rushing back into her swollen hands with a painful, tingling vengeance.

"The blindfold stays. Don't even think about it," he warned.

"I won't. Thank you," Sophie stammered, her voice trembling with manufactured obedience. She rubbed her wrists, biting back a cry as her raw skin met the chill of the air.

"Lean against the van," the man snapped. "Hurry up."

Sophie obeyed, sliding down the side of the van into a crouch. She hiked her dress as modestly as she could, adjusting her underwear to relieve the unbearable pressure in her bladder. The sound of footsteps crunching nearby sent her heart racing. *They're pacing. Good. Keep looking away.*

She used the moment of distraction to slide her hands beneath her dress, clawing at her remaining nails. The sharp sting tore through her as one acrylic wrenched down to the cuticle. She clenched her teeth against the scream clawing its way up her throat, forcing it back with shuddering breaths.

One by one, the nails came loose. *Six, maybe seven. It'll have to be enough.* She slipped them behind her heels, carefully placing them on the dirt. As she rose, she swept her foot over them, concealing them under a thin layer of soil. She made a show of adjusting her dress and flailing her arms in exaggerated movements. *Don't look down. Don't look down.*

Her victory was short-lived. Hands like iron gripped her shoulders, shoving her back into the van. This time, she sat upright, her hands free but trembling. The emptiness in her bladder and the faint hope of her hidden nails gave her a sliver of confidence. *Please find me, Izzy.*

That hope was shattered when a hand clamped over her face from behind. The sharp stench of gasoline and chemicals invaded her senses as a cloth pressed against her nose and mouth. *No. No!* She thrashed, clawing at the arms holding her, but they didn't budge. Her muffled screams filled the van, desperate and animalistic.

Air. *I need air.*

Her struggles slowed as the acrid fumes invaded her lungs, her breaths shallow and quick despite her efforts to hold them. Her vision swirled, black on black, the edges of her consciousness fading with each panicked inhale.

The last sound she heard was laughter—low, guttural, and dripping with malice. It was a sound that promised torment beyond her worst fears. As darkness claimed her, Sophie welcomed the silence, clinging to it like a fragile shield against the horror waiting for her on the other side.

CHAPTER 12

IZZY

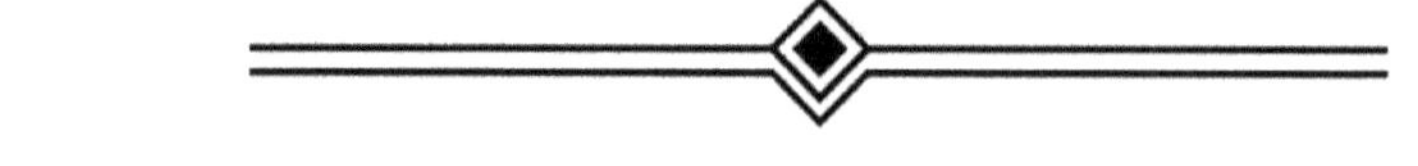

My feet pound against the earth, running. *Where am I?* The woods. The trees loom above me, their blackened silhouettes clawing at the starless sky. Shadows twist and breathe like living things, closing in from every side. My heart thunders in my chest, the rhythm echoing in my ears like a drumbeat of fear. The ground beneath me feels unstable, as if the forest itself conspires to pull me under.

I squint into the suffocating darkness, straining to see. *Please. Let me see.* But the blackness swallows everything—except for the eyes. Large, yellow, glowing like embers in the void. Watching. Waiting.

A wave of panic surges through me, and my legs scream for me to run. I try, but they feel weighted, sluggish, like I'm wading through wet cement. Each step is an agonizing effort, the trail ahead stretching endlessly into the abyss.

My lungs burn, each breath jagged and shallow, and the forest presses in closer, a predator's lair alive with menace.

The eyes emerge from the darkness, their glow illuminating a sleek, black form—a cougar. Massive, impossibly large, its body ripples with power, each movement precise and deadly. Its fur shimmers like liquid night, fangs glinting with fresh blood. A guttural growl escapes its throat, a sound so low it reverberates through my bones. My heart clenches as I realize with dawning horror: *It's not stalking me. It's already found her.*

Ahead, Sophie lies motionless on the trail. Her blonde hair spills around her pale face, her body unnervingly still. *Sophie! No!* The cougar's claws unsheath, razor-sharp, as it lunges for her. My mouth opens to scream, but no sound comes. My feet refuse to move, the leaden weight dragging me down, anchoring me in place as the beast's claws wrap around Sophie's collar.

"No," I whisper hoarsely, then louder, "No! Leave her!"

But my cries fall uselessly into the void. The cougar moves effortlessly, dragging her into the shadows with a terrifying elegance. My knees hit the dirt, my hands clawing at the ground as if I could dig a path to her. I scream again, my voice breaking with desperation.

The beast pauses, turning to face me. Its massive body shimmers, its features shifting and twisting grotesquely. Fur melts into skin, claws into hands, and suddenly, the cougar is gone. In its place stands the sandy-haired man. His eyes glow the same sickly yellow as the predator's, pupils slitted like a cat's. His grin is cruel and predatory, revealing sharp, fang-like teeth.

"Don't worry, Izzy," he drawls, his voice a low, mocking purr. "I'll take good care of her..."

The words slither through the air, cold and oily, coating me in dread. His grip tightens on Sophie's collar, and with a single jerk, he drags her further into the darkness. My body convulses with sobs, my nails digging into the unyielding earth as I try to pull myself forward. But it's no use.

The yellow eyes vanish, swallowed by the void. The forest falls silent, leaving me alone with the sound of my own wails.

I failed her. She's gone.

Izzy's eyes flew open, her heart pounding in her chest as if she'd been running for her life. For a moment, she lay frozen, expecting the yellow-eyed monster from her dream to emerge from the shadows. The room was silent, save for the faint hum of the city outside, but the vivid nightmare clung to her like a second skin. Slowly, her breathing steadied, and her mind pieced together where she was: her bedroom, the safe haven of her apartment. The clock on her nightstand blinked 5:00 AM, the numbers glowing faintly in the dimness.

Dragging her hands down her face, Izzy tried to erase the lingering images behind her eyelids—the predatory glare of those yellow eyes, the helplessness of her own body. But the weight of the dream lingered, heavy and oppressive.

Marshall stirred beside her, his hefty frame shifting under the covers. Sensing her distress, he nudged closer, his warmth grounding her in the present. She placed a hand on his head, feeling the soft rise and fall of his breath, and though his presence brought some comfort, it wasn't enough. The early morning darkness felt suffocating, and she craved light—something to chase away the remnants of that nighttime forest.

Swinging her legs over the side of the bed, she stood, grateful her body obeyed her commands with ease, unlike in her dream. The living room felt safer, bathed in the faint glow of city lights filtering through the bay window. Izzy perched herself on the sill, pulling her knees to her chest as Marshall sat alert at her side. Together, they watched the slow creep of dawn, waiting for the sun to wash away the shadows.

Despite her best efforts to distract herself, her mind raced. She'd spent the last hour brainstorming possible leads, but each idea fell flat, leaving her with a growing sense of futility. The first rays of sunlight finally broke over the horizon around 7:00 AM, streaking the sky in soft pastels. She watched the warm hues bloom against the cityscape, willing their beauty to overwrite the nightmare's hold on her.

The sound of her phone chiming broke the silence.

"You up?"

Gabe. Ever since he'd found her on the pavement outside the RidgeRunner, his texts had become a welcome constant. Sometimes they discussed leads, but other times, she suspected he just wanted to distract her—or lift her spirits. And she let him. It was nice to feel like someone cared, even if she couldn't quite understand why he did.

Izzy's fingers hovered over the keyboard before typing: "Been up for a while, couldn't sleep. Thinking about everything. You?"

His reply came almost instantly:

"Same. Maybe we'll find something new today."

She could tell the heat was already rising, and the balmy, moist air promised a pop-up storm. She was sure it was a reflection of her own mood, a squall surely on the horizon within her as well. She gazed out of her bay window, watching the occasional gust of wind sweep across the treetops with a fierce arm, the changing colors of the leaves being carried away together with each pass of the wind.

"I hope so. Thinking of taking Marshall to the park to clear my head and listen to the storm roll in. You're welcome to join if you're free?"

As soon as she sent it, a flicker of doubt crept in. Did Gabe have someone waiting for him? Surely, a man like him wouldn't be saving women and solving mysteries if he had a girlfriend—right? Focus, Izzy. Sophie is missing, and you're acting like a hormonal teenager. She shook her head and moved to the kitchen, her hands automatically reaching for the coffee pot.

Her phone buzzed again:

"I can grab coffee to fuel the brainstorming. What do you like?"

Izzy smirked as she closed the coffee pot lid. It was as if he'd read her mind.

"Cafe Americano with oat milk and hazelnut, please. And Marshall would like a cup of whipped cream :)"

"Of course, he would. Anything for the prima donna doggy."

"Gabriel, don't let him hear you say that, or he'll think you're challenging his masculinity. Grounds for a fight, if you ask me."

"I would never! Fancy coffee and whipped cream for the big, strong Marshmallow MAN dog, coming right up. Freedom Park?"

"Yep, see you there."

Izzy laughed softly, crouching to ruffle Marshall's fur. "My big, strong Marshmallow man," she cooed. He responded with a happy wag of his tail, practically bouncing with excitement when she asked, "Would you like to go to the park?" His massive frame nearly knocked her over as he leaped up, sniffing at every item she gathered for their outing.

Despite the nightmare's lingering chill, Izzy felt an unfamiliar lightness in her chest. She knew it was because of Gabe. He had a way of steadying her, though a cautious voice in the back of her mind warned against letting him too close. *We're just friends. It's only a walk in the park. What could it hurt?*

But as she finished packing her things, Izzy couldn't shake the feeling that she was lying to herself.

Izzy checked the rearview mirror one last time, her fingers smoothing down a stray lock of hair before tucking it behind her ear. The half-up style had seemed like a good idea earlier, but now she wasn't so sure. She scrutinized the soft waves, wondering if they looked effortless enough. *Not that it matters, right?* she told herself, feeling her cheeks warm as her gaze dropped to her outfit. The fitted tee and casual jeans struck the balance she wanted—relaxed, but not lazy. Still, she had to admit, it was the fourth shirt she'd tried on. *What is wrong with me?*

A wet nose nudging the side of her head broke her reverie. Marshall, unable to contain his excitement any longer, leaned forward from the backseat, sniffing her hair, ear, and neck with the enthusiasm of a dog reunited after years apart.

"Fine! I'm going, I'm going, Marshall! Quit!" Izzy squirmed away, laughing despite herself as the big fluffball nearly toppled her out of the driver's seat. With a grin, she stepped out of the car, Marshall bounding after her the moment she opened his door.

The autumn wind whipped strands of hair across her face, and she squinted against the sun's golden light. Marshall stood proudly by her side, his fur ruffling in the breeze as he waited patiently for her to clip on his leash. Once secure, he lifted his nose to the air, sniffing deeply before barking—a single, sharp announcement.

Izzy didn't need to turn to know what had caught his attention. Still, when she glanced over her shoulder, she felt the air leave her lungs.

Gabe was making his way across the parking lot, his dark curls damp and heavy, as if he'd showered just before arriving. He wore a black ribbed tank under a gray zip-up hoodie, the casual layers somehow managing to show off his muscular build. A pair of dark sunglasses perched on his nose reflected the sunlight, making it impossible to tell where his gaze landed, though she felt its weight regardless. Her eyes traveled to the scruff lining his jaw, and she clenched her hand tightly at the sudden, ridiculous urge to trace it with her fingers.

In his hands, he carried two coffee cups, steam curling softly from their lids.

Izzy swallowed and cleared her throat, her heart betraying her with its quickened rhythm. *Get it together, Izz.*

When Gabe finally reached them, he tilted his head down, peering at her over the edge of his sunglasses. His grin was easy but genuine, the kind that sent a warmth spiraling from her chest to her fingertips.

"Your Americano, milady," he said, his voice deep and smooth, with just a hint of playfulness.

She reached for the cup, her fingers brushing his in a fleeting touch that sent a spark of something electric zipping through her. Her gaze snapped up to meet his, and for a moment, she was caught in the somber depths of his eyes. They were tinged with exhaustion, yes, but also a quiet strength, as if he were carrying a weight she couldn't yet name.

Before the silence between them could grow awkward, Gabe crouched, pulling a tiny paper cup from his pocket and setting it on the pavement. "And whipped cream for the manliest of dogs."

Marshall wasted no time, diving into the treat with unrestrained joy. Izzy couldn't help but laugh as the pup's snout emerged from the cup, thoroughly coated in whipped cream. Not satisfied, Marshall nosed eagerly at Gabe's pocket and hand in search of more, eventually settling for a thorough head scratch when he came up empty. His tail wagged so furiously it was a wonder it didn't lift him off the ground.

Watching the pure, unfiltered joy on Marshall's face, Izzy felt a pang of gratitude. These small moments—Marshall's happiness, the warmth of the sun, the unexpected kindness of a near-stranger—were what kept her going.

As she sipped her coffee, savoring the rich, nutty flavor, a thought struck her, pulling her up short. *He remembered my coffee order.*

Izzy glanced at Gabe again, his grin still lingering as he stood, brushing imaginary fur off his hoodie. Her chest tightened, a mixture of gratitude and something far more dangerous swirling in her stomach.

The sun climbed higher, casting warm rays on their shoulders, though the breeze carried a forewarning of the storm to come. Leaves and branches rustled noisily overhead as they walked along the winding path that skirted the water's edge. The faint mist from the park's fountain caught on the wind, cooling their skin. Izzy inhaled deeply, the air thick with the scent of rain, refreshing and charged.

Where would they have taken her? Izzy's mind churned with possibilities, each one more dreadful than the last. *Maybe the police have an update. Should I call the detective? Will they even tell me anything?*

"What's rattling around up there, Izz?" Gabe's voice broke through her thoughts. She glanced up to find him watching her closely, his sunglasses hooked on the collar of his shirt. A passing cloud had dimmed the sunlight, and the shadows softened the sharp lines of his face. His concern was evident in the furrow of his brow, and something about his attention made her heart flutter. *It's nice...to be noticed.*

"I'm trying to figure out where I go from here, I guess." She kicked at a stray pebble on the trail, her gaze dropping to the ground. "How does someone just disappear without a trace? There has to be something, but..." Her words trailed off as she took a sip of her coffee, its subtle sweetness the only comfort she could find in the moment.

Gabe nodded, his expression thoughtful. "It's hard to feel like there's no direction. I get that." His hands slid into his pockets as he walked beside her. Marshall trotted ahead, his tail wagging with unbothered joy. "But these things take time to work out."

Izzy exhaled heavily, her frustration escaping in a single breath. "But what if she doesn't have time, Gabe?" Her voice wavered as she tilted her face toward the sky. The dark clouds now loomed closer, heavy and menacing. "I can't stand it—not knowing. It's eating me alive."

Gabe slowed his pace, his eyes softening as they met hers. "So what do you think comes next?" He drained the last of his coffee, taking her empty cup and tossing them both into a trash bin along the trail.

"I don't know." She shrugged, trying to keep her voice steady. "Maybe I'll call the detective, see if they've gotten anything out of that bartender. Who knows? Maybe they've narrowed something down." Her eyes darted away as she spoke, unwilling to let him see the uncertainty in her gaze.

"Fair place to start." Gabe's lips curved into a faint smile as he glanced skyward. His hand rose instinctively, palm up, as fat raindrops began to dot the pavement. "We should probably—"

The rain began in earnest, a sudden downpour that soaked them in seconds. They turned their faces skyward, laughing breathlessly at the absurdity of their situation.

The rain quickly escalated into a torrent, sending them sprinting toward the nearest shelter—a towering oak with a sprawling canopy. Its ancient branches seemed to beckon them, offering a reprieve from the storm.

By the time they reached the tree, Izzy was drenched, her clothes clinging to her skin. She leaned back against the rough bark, gasping for air. Gabe's momentum brought him to an abrupt halt inches from her, his hands braced against the trunk on either side of her.

The world seemed to shrink around them, the rain muffled by the thick canopy overhead. Water streamed down his face, tracing the sharp angles of his jaw and the curve of his neck. Izzy's breath hitched as her eyes lingered on his lips, glistening with rain.

Her gaze lifted to meet his, and she found the same longing reflected in his dark brown eyes. His hand rose slowly, brushing a wet strand of hair from her cheek and tucking it gently behind her ear. His fingers lingered there, light but deliberate, as if he couldn't bring himself to let go.

Her heartbeat thundered in her ears as he leaned in, his breaths mingling with hers. His lips grazed hers, featherlight, and her entire body ignited at the contact.

But the moment shattered as sirens wailed in the distance, their piercing sound cutting through the storm. They jolted apart, the spell broken.

Their eyes met again, a silent understanding passing between them. *Not now. Not like this.* Gabe's forehead rested against hers for a moment, his eyes closing as he exhaled deeply.

When he stepped back, the loss of his touch was immediate and visceral. Izzy's lips tingled, aching for what could have been. Her tongue flicked out, tasting rain and wishing it had been him.

Maybe someday.

But for now, all she could do was watch as he stepped away, his hand trailing against the rough bark before falling to his side.

"I think you're right. I need to give the police time to question their suspect," Izzy said, her voice firmer now, as if the storm had swept away her earlier doubts. "But the bartender mentioned a car, didn't he? Maybe they can track it down... or connect it to other cases. There have to be others like this. I need to call the detective."

The rain seemed to have cleared more than just the skies—it had sharpened her focus. The fog of fear and helplessness was lifting, replaced by a renewed determination. *We don't have time for hopelessness. We can't give up. Not for Sophie.*

Gabe caught on to the shift in her mood and grinned, his face lighting up in a way that momentarily made her forget the weight of everything else. As they walked, the drizzle faded to a faint mist, and the sun broke through the lingering clouds, streaking the park with light.

"I bet they can narrow it down," Gabe said, his tone teasing, "though I'm not sure I envy the poor detective who's about to get grilled with your endless questions."

Izzy rolled her eyes and gave his shoulder a playful punch, her wet hand slapping against the soaked fabric of his hoodie. Water droplets sprayed off him, and he exaggeratedly flinched away, pretending to cower from her weak blow.

She smirked, shaking her head as he laughed, the sound warm and infectious.

He glanced at her, still grinning. "I've got a few hours of work this afternoon, but you'll call me if anything comes up?" His brow arched as he lowered his head, waiting for her reply, the intensity in his eyes doing strange things to her insides.

They had reached their cars now, Marshall trotting ahead to Izzy's vehicle, his leash taut as he wagged his tail expectantly.

"Of course," she said, fiddling with her keys and looking down for a moment. A dozen thoughts collided in her mind. Should she bring up what had almost happened beneath the oak tree? Should she let it go? The words swirled but never formed, and the silence stretched just long enough to feel loaded with meaning.

Instead, she offered, "Thank you, Gabe… for the coffee." Her tone held more weight than the simple words, and when she glanced up through lowered lashes, her lips curved into a smile she couldn't quite suppress.

His response was instantaneous, and his smile—unrestrained and entirely genuine—spread across his face like sunlight after the storm. The warmth of it reached her, suffusing her chest with something she didn't dare name.

"Thank you, Izzy… for the walk."

His words were simple, but the way he said them made her breath hitch. Before she could reply, he gave a small wave and stepped toward his car, leaving her standing there, the moment lingering like the scent of rain in the air.

CHAPTER 13

GABRIEL

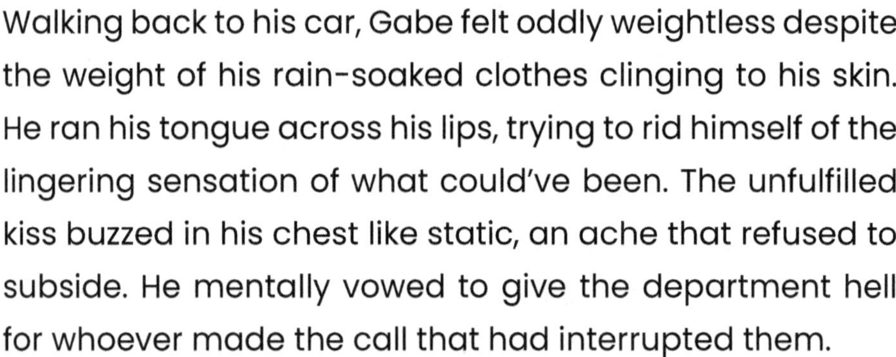

Walking back to his car, Gabe felt oddly weightless despite the weight of his rain-soaked clothes clinging to his skin. He ran his tongue across his lips, trying to rid himself of the lingering sensation of what could've been. The unfulfilled kiss buzzed in his chest like static, an ache that refused to subside. He mentally vowed to give the department hell for whoever made the call that had interrupted them.

The drive home was a blur, his thoughts a storm of frustration and longing. At a stoplight, he yanked off his drenched hoodie and tank, tossing them onto the passenger-side floorboard with a wet slap. His skin prickled in the humid air, but his mind remained locked on Izzy. That look she'd given him before they were interrupted—it hadn't been ambiguous. He knew it too well, had seen it in the mirror on the hardest days of his life.

It's impossible to pursue justice, to seek answers, and not feel selfish for wanting happiness, too.

That was how he'd lived after Finn's death—punishing himself for surviving, for his mistake. Happiness felt like a betrayal, like he hadn't earned the right to feel it. How could he, when his best friend was gone and those responsible still roamed free?

For Izzy, it wasn't quite the same. Her guilt wasn't tangled with survival, but he saw the same drive in her—a need to see justice done before she could allow herself any kind of peace. Her friend's disappearance had carved a raw wound in her soul, and she wouldn't let herself heal until Sophie was found. *If Sophie is found.* The thought hit him like a blow to the stomach, and nausea churned in his gut.

He parked outside his apartment and climbed the stairs, his body moving on autopilot. She'd texted him earlier to say she'd called the detective, but they hadn't shared much. Izzy had been adamant that the police weren't telling her everything. *She's not wrong.* He'd reassured her with the usual lines about procedures and confidentiality in an active investigation, but the truth weighed heavier than he let on.

They weren't telling her everything. And for now, that was how it had to stay.

He poured himself a fresh cup of coffee, the dark liquid steaming in the dim kitchen light. His mind flickered back to the bartender—Brandon—and Izzy's stormy reaction. Her rage had been palpable, her blue eyes flashing like a tempest. It had startled him, the sheer intensity of it. He'd been wrong to assume she was fragile. She wasn't fragile at all—she was fire and fury wrapped in a deceptively soft package.

Even so, he couldn't stop thinking about the way she'd looked at him beneath that oak tree, rain streaking down her face, her lips parted in anticipation. He felt it again, the heat igniting in his chest, but he shook it off. Focus, man.

He sent a text to Jenkins, *"has the pig squealed yet?"*

Stepping out onto his modest patio, Gabe leaned against the railing, staring out over the city. South End wasn't glamorous, but it worked for the assignment—close enough to Uptown, with just enough anonymity. The breeze carried the promise of more rain, and dark clouds gathered on the horizon, but for now, the view was peaceful.

He sipped his coffee, his dark eyes scanning the cityscape. People passed below, lost in their lives, oblivious to the shadows lurking just beyond their sight. He'd chosen this life—to stand at the edges, to protect without being seen. It was easier that way. No attachments, no questions, no one else getting hurt. That was how he'd survived after Finn. It was how he preferred it.

At least, that's what he'd thought before Izzy crashed into his life. She'd lodged herself under his skin in a matter of days, unraveling his carefully constructed solitude with her wit, her fire, and her relentless determination. He should've kept his distance. Instead, he was falling—too close, too fast.

His phone buzzed, pulling him from his thoughts. Jenkins.

"Narrowed it down to a BMW coupe, maybe an M4. You free for rendezvous? You'll need to come down to the precinct for this one."

Gabe shot back a thumbs-up emoji, his pulse quickening. Finally, a lead. Small, but it was something.

Draining the rest of his coffee, he rinsed the mug and grabbed his keys. As the adrenaline kicked in, he felt a familiar rush—part excitement, part dread. The chase was on, and he wasn't about to let this one slip through his fingers.

Parking several blocks away in an inconspicuous alley, Gabe scanned the street for any wandering eyes before stepping onto the sidewalk. The morning was quiet, foot traffic sparse, the city still waking up. Crossing a couple of streets, he ducked into a side walkway and approached the back entrance of the police department. *We really need more tree coverage out here.*

Flashing a badge from under his shirt, Gabe passed through the security checkpoint and into the back hallway. The building's modern design, all sharp edges and clean lines, felt sterile. Sunlight streamed through towering glass windows in the lobby, highlighting the flag displays but doing little to warm the cold atmosphere. The muted tones of gray and white cast a pall over the bustling conversations around him. Gabe kept his head down, avoiding eye contact. The whispers and sideways glances from familiar faces didn't escape him, but he refused to give them power. *They're probably rehashing my failures. Fine, let them. I don't care.*

Reaching Jenkins' cubicle, Gabe straightened, his steps quickening with purpose. His mind buzzed with the possibilities, the promise of progress. *A lead. Finally.* But his voice came out rougher than he intended.

"This better be good to have me come all the way in here."

Jenkins barely flinched at his tone, already used to Gabe's gruff exterior. "Yeah, yeah, it is. And it's a little complicated, so I wanted you to see the footage firsthand."

Sliding into his chair, Jenkins began clicking through files, pulling up several screens on his dual monitors. "Our guy, Brandon, narrowed it down for us. Turns out threatening him with life in the worst prison on the East Coast made him a little more cooperative. He couldn't ID the exact model but said it's probably a brand-new BMW coupe. An M4, if he had to guess. Not a scratch on it."

Jenkins pulled up a snapshot from a traffic camera. "This was taken right around the corner from the RidgeRunner. Our guy ran a red light. See the timestamp?" He pointed to the corner of the screen. Six minutes after Sophie was last seen leaving the club.

Gabe muttered a curse under his breath, leaning in to study the image. "What else? License plate? Owner?" His questions spilled out, laced with urgency. *A lead this thin could snap at any second.*

"At first, not much," Jenkins admitted, pulling up another screen. The grainy footage showed the mouth of a side street. "The plate's registered to a trailer park outside the city. Checked it this morning—car's not there anymore, probably under a fake name, but we're running it. Then I ran the plate through other footage we have. This alley was part of a drug bust last month, and they never took down the feed."

Jenkins clicked to the next clip. The BMW sped into the narrow backstreet. A gray cargo van—plain, forgettable—sped out from the opposite end of the same alley.

Gabe's jaw clenched as he ran his hand through his damp hair, memorizing every detail of the van: the license plate, the shape, the grime streaks on its sides. His pulse quickened. *This has to be it. It's too clean, too deliberate.*

"That's got to be our girl," Gabe said, his voice low, his body coiled with tension. The heat in his ears spread through him, his fingers twitching with the need to act.

"It's a strong lead," Jenkins agreed. "Last traffic cam caught them headed north on I-77. Toward the lake."

Gabe stared at him, his patience fraying. "So a team's en route?"

Jenkins hesitated, his mouth flattening into a thin line. "You know how these guys are. Too much noise, too fast, and they'll bolt. We can't risk spooking them."

Gabe exhaled sharply, his frustration mounting. *Always the same. Play it safe, keep the protocol. Meanwhile, she's out there.* He yanked his keys from his pocket.

"Fine. I'll pursue. Can I at least get some backup in the area?" He didn't wait for a reply, already turning on his heel.

"Of course. I'll have uniforms in the vicinity. Keep me updated," Jenkins called after him. His tone was steady, but the unspoken worry lingered in the air: *Just in case it all goes to hell.*

Gabe's steps quickened as he exited the building, his adrenaline surging. The familiar rhythm of the chase gripped him, sharpening his focus. This was his world— tracking shadows, chasing ghosts, pushing forward with nothing but a gut feeling and raw determination.

We're close, Sophie. Hold on.

Gabe wasn't entirely sure why he'd called Izzy. Maybe it was the morning spent walking with her, the ease of her presence, or maybe it was the growing sense that he wanted her near. When Jenkins had suggested he pursue the lead on the van, his mind had conjured only one image—Izzy in the passenger seat, sharp-eyed and relentless. *This girl is under my skin.*

But whatever impulse had driven him, he regretted it almost immediately. His text had been simple—*"I have a lead. Pick you up in twenty."* Yet, from the moment she'd appeared in the doorway, she'd practically tackled him with questions.

Her inquiries were sharp, her logic piercing, and worse, painfully relevant. Questions he couldn't answer. Questions that would demand truths he wasn't ready to share. "Do you trust me, Izz?" he'd finally asked, a weak deflection, even in his own mind.

Her reply had come after a long pause. "Yeah... I do."

That hesitant trust hit him like a punch to the gut. She didn't have all the facts, yet she was still placing her faith in him. He could see the questions burning in her blue eyes, but she didn't press him further. Guilt surged, sharp and immediate. *She's too close. Too damn close.*

He turned the key in the ignition, and they set off, the silence between them heavy with unspoken tension. But he could feel her eyes on him, dissecting him, waiting for cracks to appear.

"So, let me get this straight," she began, her voice directed at the window but edged with exasperation. "Our only hope for finding my friend is sitting in a cell, and now you suddenly have a secret lead that you can't explain? But you know it's urgent?"

Gabe gripped the wheel tighter. He said nothing, forcing himself to focus on the road ahead.

"And Lake Norman?" she continued, her tone rising. "Do you realize how big it is? All the little coves and inlets? Sure, Brandon said something about the lake, but narrowing it down—"

"It's worth a look," he cut her off, his voice clipped.

She fell silent, her frustration palpable. He could feel the weight of her glare, even as he kept his own gaze fixed ahead. *She's not wrong. Damn it, she's not wrong.* But he couldn't let her pick apart the thin threads of his lead. Not now.

Minutes passed, thick with tension, as the highway stretched out before them. Gabe turned off at an exit leading north, toward the last known direction of the van. The air in the car was taut with unspoken thoughts, but when he glanced over, Izzy had shifted her focus to the horizon, her eyes scanning with sharp intent.

She'd stopped questioning him—for now. The need to find Sophie, to uncover anything that might bring her closer to her friend, outweighed her desire for answers from him.

As they neared a dirt road that veered sharply off the main route, something caught Gabe's attention. Fresh tire marks cut deep into the earth, their abrupt stop sending a chill through him. He slowed the car.

Izzy noticed it too. The car rolled to a halt, and her questioning eyes turned to him. Gabe avoided her gaze, stepping out of the vehicle. "Try not to disturb anything," he warned, his voice firm. "They might be able to use it for evidence."

Izzy followed close behind as they traced the tracks, her tension palpable. The path led into a cluster of trees, hidden from the road. And then she froze.

"Gabe…" Her voice broke, trembling with emotion. "These are—oh my God, these are hers."

Before them lay a small pile of acrylic fingernails, scattered and trampled into the dirt. Blood, dark and dried, clung to the edges of some. Izzy knelt, reaching out instinctively, but Gabe's hand shot out to stop her.

"Izzy, stop!" His voice was sharp, almost panicked. "Don't touch anything. We need to call the police."

Izzy spun on him, her face a storm of anguish and fury. "Oh, now we need to call the police, Gabe? What the hell is going on with you? How did you know she was brought here? And what's with all this 'don't touch anything' crap?"

Her voice rose with each word, her anger spilling over. "What aren't you telling me?!"

Gabe stepped back, his hands raised in a placating gesture. *She's right to be angry.* Her words hit like blows, each one a reminder of the secrets he was keeping, the truths he couldn't share.

"Izz," he began, his voice softer now, almost apologetic. "We need to talk."

CHAPTER 14

I can't believe I trusted him so easily.

The thought hit like a dagger, twisting deeper with every step. Her breath quickened as she stomped through the woods, each step heavy with fury.

He looked through my underwear.

A fresh wave of heat surged to her face, half mortification, half anger. Gabe must think she was naïve—a silly, clueless girl playing at being an investigator. *I don't CARE what he thinks!* The lie burned her, almost as much as the truth. She did care. More than she wanted to admit.

It all made sense now. The police hadn't rushed to collect the footage because *he already had it.* He wasn't some good Samaritan who stayed at the hospital because he didn't like leaving her alone—he had an agenda. Everyone has an angle. *And I fell for it.*

Her pace quickened, her fury building with each memory. She thought of the late-night ice cream, his easy smiles, and the unspoken connection she'd felt. *I invited him over like a lovesick idiot. He must think I'm pathetic.* Her chest tightened with the weight of her humiliation.

But beneath the anger and embarrassment, another emotion lingered, coiling in the pit of her stomach: hurt.

Gabe had explained everything—or so he claimed. Izzy replayed his words in her mind, the tightness in her chest refusing to ease.

"Undercover police work is all about gaining trust," he'd said, his hands raised as if begging forgiveness. "I hated lying to you, Izz. I really did."

He'd told her about the missing women, about how Sophie's case wasn't an isolated incident. Three others. Three lives snuffed out, with no closure for their families. He'd recounted the RidgeRunner's connection to the disappearances, his cover as a driver, and the coincidence of being the one to find her that night.

It all made sense. Too much sense. And yet, it didn't absolve him.

Her voice cracked as she whispered, "You lied to me."

"I had to. It's my job." His brown eyes had pleaded with her, filled with regret and something else—something she wasn't ready to believe. "I didn't want to, Izzy. You have to know that."

But did she? Could she ever trust someone like him again? Someone whose entire life depended on deception?

The woods pressed in around her, the gnarled branches clawing at her jacket as she stormed toward the road. Her thoughts tangled like vines, tightening their grip with each passing moment. *He didn't need me. Not really. I was a pawn. A convenient cover.*

A scoff escaped her lips, bitter and sharp. She thought of how he'd stood by her side, how he'd listened to her, how he'd made her feel seen. Was that all part of the act? *Even the story about his best friend... was that a lie too?*

She blinked back tears, her vision blurring as she pushed through the underbrush. *I'm such a fool.*

Embarrassment flooded her so fully, that her skin felt tight and flushed. Standing in that copse of trees, surrounded by all those uniformed bodies, moving around, she felt stripped bare. The urge to run, to be *anywhere* else, was a physical force driving her feet to escape. By the time she reached the road, her legs trembled with the weight of the day, but she refused to stop. Gabe's car sat where they'd parked, the keys still in the ignition. Without hesitation, she climbed in and turned the engine over.

The drive back to her apartment felt surreal. The eviction notice still clung to her door like a cruel reminder of her crumbling life. She stared at it, her heart hollow. It had only been a few days since she'd found it, but the weight of everything that had happened since made it feel like a lifetime ago.

Her hands trembled as she gripped the steering wheel. The fight drained from her, replaced by an overwhelming wave of grief. The sob came unbidden, ripping from her throat in a burst of sound that echoed through the car.

Why do I lose everyone?

Her head fell to the wheel, her tears spilling onto her lap. The answer she'd buried for so long clawed its way to the surface: *It's me. I'm the problem.*

When the tears finally subsided, Izzy pulled out her phone. Her fingers hovered over the screen for a moment before typing a message:

"Have your buddies give you a ride. Your car is at the apartment."

It was cruel, and she felt a pang of guilt as she hit send. But the ache in her chest was louder than her conscience. She couldn't bear to face him again. *Not now. Not after this.*

Shoving her phone into her pocket, she stepped out of the car and into the stillness of her apartment. The air felt heavy, pressing down on her as she moved to the couch. She sat, her body sinking into the worn cushions as her thoughts spiraled.

I wanted to trust him. I needed to.

Her eyes burned with fresh tears, but she refused to let them fall. *I thought I needed him.*

The truth was harder to face. What she'd needed was hope. Gabe had offered that, even if it was built on lies. And now, with every piece of her life in shambles, she wasn't sure she could pick up the pieces alone.

But I have to. I always have.

As always, when her thoughts turned chaotic, Izzy turned to the mountains. The familiar weight of her pack and the steady presence of Marshall provided the only solace she could rely on. Today, she chose a path more remote and treacherous than her usual hikes. It wasn't just a need for escape—it was a challenge she needed to conquer. Something to remind her she could overcome obstacles, even as the weight of betrayal threatened to crush her.

The narrow trail snaked along precarious cliffs, its edges falling into a dizzying abyss. Ancient roots clawed their way out of the ground, ready to trip the careless. Every step required precision, every movement a careful calculation. The sun barely penetrated the dense canopy, its light fragmented into dappled patterns on the mossy ground.

The air was crisp and earthy, a sharp contrast to the heavy, humid atmosphere of the city she'd left behind.

Each breath she took was ragged, not only from exertion but from the emotional storm raging within her. *I'm not weak. I won't let this define me. I don't need him to find Sophie.* The thought spurred her forward, her resolve hardening with every step.

Marshall trailed her at first, his head low and watchful. But when a rabbit darted across their path, his instincts overtook him. He bolted, a white blur crashing through the underbrush.

"Marshall! No!" Izzy yelled, frustration surging through her. Of course, she'd forgotten his leash. It was a rookie mistake, one she couldn't afford right now. She muttered a curse under her breath, sprinting after him.

The trail vanished beneath her boots as she chased Marshall's retreating form into the wilderness. She reached into her pack for neon twine, tying it to low-hanging branches as she went. Her pulse raced, her shouts echoing off the trees. The thick woods seemed to close in around her, their silence oppressive, broken only by the occasional rustle of unseen animals.

The land began to slope downward, and she skidded to a halt at the edge of a clearing. A fence cut through the undergrowth, its weathered wood blending into the wild surroundings. Beyond it, a cottage clung to the mountainside, a relic of another time. Its leaning structure was held together by thick ropes of vines, the wood darkened by years of rain and decay. It seemed abandoned—until she saw the shotgun.

The muzzle pointed directly at her chest. Izzy froze, her hands shooting up instinctively.

"Please!" Her voice trembled despite her efforts to keep calm. "I'm just looking for my dog! He ran off—I don't mean any harm."

The woman holding the gun stepped closer, her wiry frame silhouetted against the cottage. She moved with the deliberate caution of someone unaccustomed to visitors, her gnarled hands steady on the weapon. Her face was a roadmap of wrinkles, each line etched by years of sun, wind, and solitude.

The barrel dipped slightly, though suspicion lingered in the woman's sharp eyes. "Round here somewhere. Nosing around the chickens, I reckon." Her voice was soft but firm, her Appalachian accent wrapping around the words like the rhythm of an old song.

Relief washed over Izzy as she lowered her arms, following the woman around the side of the cottage. "Thank you. I'm Izzy, by the way." Her voice was still shaky, but the tension in her chest began to ease.

"Maggie," the woman replied simply.

Izzy could have collapsed with relief if she weren't still in shock at the unlikelihood of her happening upon such a place in the vastness of the mountains. She took in the sight with wonder: chickens peppered a fenced area with long grass, while a couple of goats gnawed at another patch of greenery and weeds beyond them. The front of the shack was adorned with a small porch, some timbers repaired with unhewn logs. A single chair, clearly handmade, sat sturdily on it. A woodpile lay stacked neatly against the side of the porch's awning, protecting it from the weather. Leaning against it was an ax, sharp and gleaming. She wondered briefly if this woman was truly capable of maintaining all this by herself, but the lonesome porch chair seemed to glare at her in answer.

The sight of Marshall bounding around the chicken coop, his tail wagging enthusiastically, nearly brought Izzy to tears. "You're lucky you're cute," she muttered, clipping his leash to his collar.

The woman eyed Izzy as she inspected her property. "Grab your pup there and come on in to warm yer bones. A storm's comin' in quick."

Izzy hesitated, glancing at the sky. The first drops of rain began to fall, cool against her flushed skin. The timing was uncanny, as if Maggie had summoned the storm herself. Chickens clucked lazily in the coop, unfazed by the rain. Maggie opened the door, the scent of wood smoke wafting out.

Marshall tugged on the leash, eager to explore. Izzy followed, casting one last glance at the storm-darkened sky. Something about this place, about Maggie, felt otherworldly—ancient and powerful, like the mountains themselves. She stepped inside, wondering what she'd stumbled into.

Inside, the shack surprised Izzy. It was far cleaner than the weathered exterior suggested. Though the structure was run-down, there was an orderliness to the space that spoke to its inhabitant's resilience. A basket of eggs, their shells painted in earthy tones, rested on a worn wooden counter. Strands of drying herbs hung from the ceiling, their fragrance blending with the wood smoke curling from a cast-iron stove in the corner.

Maggie moved with quiet efficiency, pouring steaming water into two mismatched mugs. "Tea's almost ready," she said firmly, her tone leaving no room for debate. "We'll have a cup, then you can tell me what really brought you to these woods."

Izzy accepted the tea cautiously, waiting until Maggie drank from her own cup before taking a sip. The brew was earthy and rich, the sharpness of spearmint softened by the warmth of chamomile. It soothed her frayed nerves, but Maggie's expectant gaze quickly brought her tension back.

Izzy explained that Marshall's usual demeanor was to stay close, but his obsession with fluffy bunnies sometimes outweighed his concern for her. Thinking her story concluded, Izzy sipped her tea, cautious against its heat.

Still, Maggie looked at her expectantly. "That's how you got here. But what brings you here?" She gestured vaguely toward the dense forest beyond the clouded window, her meaning clear.

Izzy hesitated, caught off guard by the question's weight. "Ah, that's a long story," she said, attempting a polite smile that quickly faltered. "I'm not sure you've got the time, or I've got the energy." Her gaze dropped to the cracked surface of the mug.

But Maggie remained silent, her knowing eyes fixed on Izzy, peeling back layers of pretense. The silence pressed against her, and Izzy felt compelled to answer.

"Let's just say I've got some ghosts I'm trying to outrun," she admitted quietly. "The mountains... they've always felt like the place to do that." She paused, sighing. "But today, I got ahead of myself."

Maggie nodded, the motion slow and deliberate, but her eyes darkened. "Your kind of ghosts, sure," she said. "But you can't outrun 'em. You gotta face 'em head-on, or they'll find you out." Her voice lowered. "And as for the more real kind of nightwalkin' creatures, you won't escape them in these mountains."

Izzy gave a small, incredulous laugh. "I suppose there are all sorts of animals out here to watch for."

"I didn't say animals, girl." Maggie's tone sharpened, and Izzy's smile faded. The older woman puffed on a pipe she had packed, her expression unreadable. "Not all creatures of the night have fangs. Wolves in these parts hunt more than lambs, and the ones they take never come back."

Izzy swallowed, the ominous words settling like a stone in her chest. Her heartbeat quickened. *Could Sophie be here? Hidden in these woods?*

"Maggie..." Izzy's voice cracked, but she pressed on. "Are you saying there are people held captive in these mountains?"

The older woman studied her for a long moment, her weathered face unreadable. "Seems to me," Maggie said finally, "sometimes running from ghosts looks a lot like searching for something else."

Izzy's patience thinned, but she forced herself to stay calm. "I'm looking for someone, Maggie—my best friend, Sophie. She was..." Her throat tightened. "She was taken. Do you know where she might be?"

Maggie's eyes narrowed, her posture shifting slightly. "If she's in these woods, it's not safe for her. Or for you."

"Please," Izzy whispered. "If you know anything, tell me."

Maggie sighed, relenting. "There's a place. Darker than dark. Even the creatures with fangs avoid it. A den for wolves who don't leave footprints." Her voice dropped to a near-whisper. "A ramshackle cabin near the mouth of an old cave. Ain't no place for wanderers. Those who've gone in... never come out."

Izzy's breath caught, her mind racing. A cabin. A cave. Hidden, but real. This is it. *This has to be it.*

The air outside the cottage smelled of rain. Maggie's warning echoed in Izzy's ears as she secured Marshall's leash and thanked the woman. "They won't hold her there long," Maggie had said. "They'll move her soon. If you're gonna do something, girl, do it fast. But don't go alone."

Izzy promised she'd seek help, though her resolve had already formed. *I won't wait. Sophie doesn't have time.*

Retracing her steps with the help of the neon twine, Izzy found the trail and paused to send a message:

"9-1-1. I think I know where she is. Please send help."

She attached her location and Maggie's description of the cabin near the cave. Then she hit send, holding the phone skyward until the signal strengthened and the message went through.

Sorry, Maggie. I said I'd ask for help. I never said I'd wait for it.

Turning toward the path Maggie had described, Izzy adjusted her pack and gripped the straps tightly. Her determination burned brighter than her fear. *Hang on, Sophie. I'm coming.*

CHAPTER 15

GABRIEL

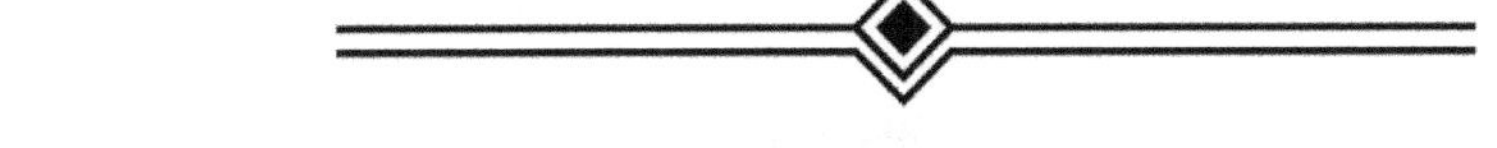

"9-1-1, I think I know where she is. They'll move her soon. Please send help."

The text hit Gabe like a punch to the gut. For a split second, his mind blanked, and then came the sinking realization: She's going after them alone.

His fingers tightened around the phone as he reread the message, dread mounting with every word. He thought giving her space after their fight was the right thing to do, giving her time to cool off and process everything he'd told her. He'd underestimated her—again. Of course, Izzy wasn't the type to sit back and wait, especially not when her best friend's life was hanging in the balance.

I should've known better.

Another ping drew his attention, the text containing coordinates and a set of directions leading to a remote section of woods. Gabe swiped to the map and toggled to satellite view. The area was dense and mountainous, with barely a trail to speak of. It was the kind of place no one stumbled upon by accident—the perfect location for captors to lie low, far from watchful eyes.

She's serious. She's really going in. Alone.

Gabe swore under his breath, frustration and fear coiling tight in his chest. How did she find this? The department had the only actionable evidence—or so he'd thought. Somehow, Izzy had managed to uncover something they'd missed. His lips twitched in a grim, bitter smile. You never stop surprising me, Izz.

But her determination to act on her own wasn't just reckless—it was dangerous. His pulse spiked at the thought of her wandering into an unknown situation with nothing but her courage and anger to guide her.

Gabe hit Jenkins' number on speed dial. The second his handler picked up, Gabe barked, "We've got a lead. Izzy's heading straight into it, solo. We need everything—SWAT, air support, the works."

There was no hesitation on Jenkins' end. Gabe's tone alone made it clear this wasn't a drill. "Coordinates?"

Gabe rattled off the details from Izzy's message, pacing as he talked, his mind racing through the logistics. The mountains were dense, trails narrow, and the clock was ticking.

"We'll be moving in an hour," Jenkins confirmed.

"Not soon enough," Gabe muttered. Every second felt like an eternity.

"Gabe," Jenkins said, his tone weighted, "you need to stay sharp. No room for errors."

"Understood," Gabe replied, though the memories clawed at the edges of his mind. SWAT, the coordinated chaos, the fateful night Finn had been taken from him. The same kind of mission. The same stakes. The same crushing responsibility.

But this time, failure wasn't an option. Izzy's life was on the line, along with Sophie's and who knew how many others.

As Gabe ended the call, a surge of adrenaline flooded his system, steeling his resolve. He didn't have time to dwell on what had been, only what needed to be done. He grabbed his gear and moved with purpose.

His car roared to life, tires screeching as he sped toward the meeting point. Despite the rush, his mind remained locked on Izzy. He'd asked her once if she trusted him. Against all odds, she'd said yes. Now, he had to return that trust, no matter how reckless her actions seemed.

But guilt gnawed at him, sharp and unrelenting. If only she'd stayed long enough to hear him out after the fight. To understand that every lie he'd told, every omission, had been a calculated move to protect the investigation—and her. But how could she see that when all she'd known was his betrayal?

His grip on the wheel tightened as he pushed the car harder. This wasn't just about Sophie anymore. It was about Izzy, too. She'd entrusted him with her fight, with her friend's life, and now it was his turn to prove he was worthy of that trust.

"Hold on, Izz," he muttered, his voice low and raw. "Just hold on."

1 month after Finn's death

Dr. Evelyn Byrne sat in her plush red chair, her glasses resting atop her nose. A padfolio lay in her lap, prepared for whatever secrets her client may lay bare. She observed Gabe across from her, his leg crossed at the ankle, and his arm draped over the back of the modern gray couch. He was the picture of confidence, undeterred by being mandated to attend this session. The room was tense with a heavy silence. The clock ticked impatiently on the wall. Gabe was sure it was a tactic to get him to speak, and he didn't intend to crack that easily.

"Officer Walsh," Dr. Byrne began gently, "do you know why you've been asked to see me today?" Her head cocked subtly as if craning to hear his response.

Gabe's jaw twitched as he replied. "Cause I lost my partner." His eyes rolled, his annoyance clear.

"While I would normally agree," she said, lifting the top sheet of her notes, "your Captain expresses concerns that you openly display anger, lack self-control, and have impaired decision-making ability." She let the silence hang for a beat before continuing. "Would you consider this a fair assessment of your recent behavior?"

Gabe smirked, knowing full well the incident that had landed him here. Yesterday, a mouthy rookie got cocky running his mouth while Gabe was filing reports. A comment about Gabe's *aim* had landed flatly behind his back among a group of officers. Still, the rookie wouldn't let up, and despite Gabe's warning, he didn't take the hint. Thanks to a couple of healing stitches, he won't be running his mouth for a while.

"I suppose it's all about the wording," Gabe responded smugly.

"And how would you *word* it, Officer Walsh?" She studied him, her hand resting thoughtfully on her chin, a pen between her fingers.

Gabe sighed, rubbing his eyes, frustrated at having to leave his work—his *real* work—to sit here while his every thought was dissected. As if his grief were something abnormal. "I don't know, *Doctor.* I guess I reacted."

"Have you considered that the way you choose to react is what is concerning?" She raised her eyebrows together in concern, awaiting his response. He stayed quiet, only looking at her with a *what do you want from me* look on his face.

"Okay then, let's go back to the case that sparked all of this. Tell me about how the case began."

When Gabe hesitated, his frustration nearly bubbling over, Dr. Byrne added, "If needed, I can remind you that your return to duty does depend on your participation here today."

Gabe sighed heavily, steeling himself to talk about the things he very clearly did not want to discuss. "The case. Started with an increase in missing persons—particularly young, attractive women—in the South Charlotte area. Investigators narrowed it down to a particular district they suspected the women might be held in. It was a house on the outskirts—looked abandoned, but people in the area reported suspicious activity. Late-night comings and goings, odd noises, that sort of thing.

"After confirming the presence of our suspects, SWAT was called to seize the building and recover any hostages. During the..." Gabe's voice faltered, the emotion thickening in his throat as he approached the tumultuous portion of the tale. He continued, "During the raid, I missed a suspect in the initial sweep. The bullet that was meant for me hit my partner, Finn. He was in intensive care for four days before succumbing to his injuries."

He couldn't bring himself to say dying, though the word hung in the air between them.

"Only one suspect was apprehended in the firefight, though all the hostages were recovered. The department suspects the rest of the group has set up shop elsewhere in the city."

Once Gabe finished recounting the events, a wave of nausea rolled through his gut, as it always did when he thought of those men still out there—free to continue their crimes.

"A very clinical assessment, Officer Walsh. But I want to know more about your perspective – what you *felt* about the case." If he didn't know better, he might think the doctor was getting exasperated with him, too. *I can't blame her. I know I'm not making this easy.*

"I don't think I had any *feelings* toward the case until the raid went bad. The guys were lowlifes, and we were there to take them down. That was it." Gabe crossed his arms, knowing she'd conclude that he was being guarded, and he didn't care.

"Okay, and when it went bad, as you said, what did you feel then?" She waited.

"What did I *feel* when I screwed up as a point man, missed a perp, and my partner died because of it?" His voice rose, raw and edged with anger. "I would say I felt pretty *bad*, doc. Is that what you want to hear?" His hands curled into fists, his knuckles whitening. The pressure in his chest built to an unbearable weight. His voice cracked as he continued, "That bullet should've been mine. I messed up, and Finn paid the price. He was good—better than me. If anyone should be gone, it's me."

Dr. Byrne didn't speak right away. When she finally did, her voice was calm but firm. "I'm not going to waste time with clichés, Walsh. But if you believe Finn should've had the time you were given, then I'd challenge you to consider: what would Finn do with that time? Would he be beating up rookies with big mouths?" She smirked, eyebrows raised, knowing she'd hit her mark.

Her words hit him like a gut punch. Gabe's anger deflated, replaced by something he couldn't quite name. Finn wouldn't have wasted a second. He'd have thrown himself into the work, doing everything in his power to stop the bastards who took those women—and his life.

Gabe leaned forward, resting his elbows on his knees. For the first time, he met Dr. Byrne's eyes. "You're right," he said quietly, the spark of an idea igniting in his mind. "Maybe it's time for a transfer."

"To where?" she asked, her tone curious.

"Special Investigations," he said, the conviction in his voice growing stronger.

LIAM

The Day of the Accident

Liam stepped out of the restaurant onto East Boulevard, the golden hues of the evening light giving way to the electric buzz of the city at night. The dinner crowds thinned as he made his way toward his car, the murmur of conversations fading into the background. Normally, a meal and a few drinks were enough to drown his thoughts for a while, but tonight was different. The nagging sensation of being watched clung to him like a shadow.

I'm in deep this time.

The neon lights from nearby bars cast warped reflections onto the wet pavement, painting the street in shifting patches of red and blue. Liam quickened his pace, but the prickle on the back of his neck only grew sharper. The cocaine was gone—vanished into the chaos of some party—and there was no way to get it back. They were waiting for him; he could feel it.

As he passed an alley, his instincts screamed too late. Figures emerged from the darkness, their silhouettes hard-edged and purposeful. Liam turned to run, but they were on him before he could take a step.

Hands grabbed him, iron-strong and unrelenting, forcing him to his knees on the filthy concrete. The first punch came fast, a sharp explosion of pain in his side, stealing his breath. Another followed, and then another, until he was left gasping, saliva and blood dripping from his mouth. Two men hauled him upright, their grips bruising, while his legs trembled beneath him.

A taller man stepped forward, his face illuminated briefly by the flicker of a neon sign. A jagged scar carved its way down the left side of his face, disappearing into the tattooed expanse of his neck. His shaved head gleamed under the light, and his eyes—cold and pitiless—pinned Liam where he stood.

"Where's the money for the blow, Liam?" the man asked, his voice low and venomous.

Liam's stomach churned. He hadn't seen this man before, but he knew the type—just another link in the chain of a labyrinthine operation designed to keep people like him confused and expendable. His mind raced, but there was no excuse that would save him.

"I told your boss," Liam gasped, his voice shaky. "It… it was a party. I don't know what happened. It got used up. Stolen. I swear, I'll get the money. I just need time."

The scarred man chuckled, the sound devoid of humor. "That's not how this works, kid. You don't lose a kilo of our coke and walk away." He flexed his thick fingers, the rings on them catching the light and drawing Liam's eyes to the scarred knuckles beneath.

The sight made Liam shudder. He knew the knuckles weren't for decoration. His gaze shifted, catching the glint of a gun tucked into the man's waistband. The nausea surged. "Please," Liam stammered, his voice barely above a whisper. "I'll get the money. I swear. Just give me a little time."

The man stepped closer, his breath hot and foul as he leaned down to meet Liam's eye. "That's what I like about you, pretty boy—all those connections. Keep our names out of your mouth, explain whatever you need to Mommy and Daddy, but you've got three days. You don't show up with our money?" He grinned, his teeth bared like a predator's. "Say your goodbyes."

Liam nodded furiously, his body trembling with equal parts fear and relief. They were going to let him go—this time. The men shoved him toward the end of the alley, his knees nearly buckling as he staggered forward. The deal was struck: three days to scrape together the cash or face consequences he didn't dare imagine.

But as he stumbled onto the sidewalk, he realized the enormity of his predicament. His parents, wealthy and privileged, believed their money could solve any problem. But he couldn't tell them the truth. He knew what would happen: they'd go to the police, and the men would make good on their threats. He'd be dead before the ink dried on the paperwork.

Without the truth, though? He wasn't sure they'd give him a dime. Not the kind of money he needed.

The weight of it all pressed down on him, his breath coming in shallow gasps as he leaned against a lamppost. *I'm screwed.*

Arriving at the apartment, Liam's mind churned with desperate possibilities, each more futile than the last. Tell Mom and Dad the truth? They'd get the police involved, and I'd be dead by morning. Withdraw a fortune from their accounts and hope they don't notice? No chance. Convince my friends to cough up money for all the coke they snorted? Laughable. Escape? They'd hunt me down.

He stopped in the living room, tossing his jacket onto the back of a chair. Isabelle was sitting on the couch, her knees pulled to her chest, her face streaked with dried tears. Her red-rimmed eyes locked on him, filled with something between fear and sorrow. His gut tightened at the sight. I don't have time for this.

"What's wrong, Isabelle?" His voice was sharp, clipped, the words coming out before he could temper them. His mind was still in that alley, replaying every blow and every threat. But the answer came swiftly, and it wasn't one he was prepared for.

She placed a pregnancy test on the coffee table, her hand trembling as she withdrew it.

Liam froze. No. Hell no. His stomach dropped, heat rising to his face. For a moment, he couldn't even breathe. This wasn't real. This couldn't be real. He'd barely managed to scrape through the alley alive, and now this? His mind screamed for escape.

"What the hell is that?!" he snapped, his voice louder than intended, anger surging to the surface like a breaking wave. *If my parents find out, I'll lose any shot at getting the money. No way I'm getting tied down here. Not now. Not ever.*

The tires of Liam's Jaguar XF screeched as he sped away from the apartment, the sharp sting of Isabelle's parting words still echoing in his mind. "Get out." She'd thrown him out of the apartment he paid for, her tears and anger burning in his memory like cigarette ash on skin. He clenched the steering wheel, trying to bury his frustration beneath the hum of the engine. *She'll figure it out. She always does.*

The Jaguar, Firenze red with sleek black leather interior, was his pride—a gift from his parents, who were eager to reward his shallow promise to join the family business. It handled like a dream, hugging the curves of the highway as if it were born to race. *A pity they weren't as thrilled about the speeding tickets, but this car was meant to be driven, not coddled.*

The golden light of twilight bathed the road ahead in an almost ethereal glow, and for a moment, Liam felt untouchable. He pushed the car harder, the speedometer climbing steadily as the asphalt stretched endlessly before him. His thoughts returned to the alley, to the scarred man's face, to the crushing realization that he was utterly trapped. His hand instinctively reached into his pocket, retrieving the mint tin he always kept close. The tiny bump of cocaine he inhaled jolted through his system like lightning, sharpening his focus and dulling the edges of his fear.

92... 96... 100... *Faster. Faster.*

At 112 mph, the deer appeared like an apparition, its antlers stark against the darkening horizon. Liam's body reacted before his mind could catch up. He yanked the wheel to the left, narrowly clipping the deer with the front fender. The sickening crunch of metal and bone echoed through the car, and in an instant, all control was lost.

The Jaguar veered sharply, the tires screeching in protest before the car slammed into the guardrail. The impact was deafening, shattering the windshield as Liam was hurled forward. Time slowed as his body sailed through the air, suspended between the fractured twilight above and the black waters below.

Pain didn't register, not at first. Only the surreal sensation of falling, his mind struggling to reconcile what had happened. Then the water hit—cold, suffocating, and unrelenting.

For a moment, everything was still. The Jaguar sank beneath him, its crumpled frame disappearing into the depths of the lake. The silence pressed against his eardrums, and his lungs burned for air. Panic surged as he kicked toward the surface, gasping desperately when he broke free.

Dripping and winded, Liam hauled himself onto the muddy north shore, the adrenaline coursing through his veins the only thing keeping him moving. His limbs ached, every joint and muscle screaming in protest, but his mind was alive with a singular, wild thought: *What if I don't go back?*

The idea expanded, taking root as he looked back toward the wreckage. The mangled remains of the overpass loomed in the distance, tendrils of metal and concrete silhouetted against the dim light. *If they think I'm dead, they won't come after me.*

The thought gave him a burst of clarity. He wasn't sure where he'd go, but the cabin in the mountains seemed like a logical choice. Remote. Isolated. The perfect place to disappear.

Rain began to fall as Liam stumbled toward the treeline, his body running on borrowed time and chemicals. His shoes squelched against the muddy ground, but he didn't stop. He couldn't stop. The weight of his situation bore down on him, but for the first time, a spark of hope flared against the darkness.

I'm not dead yet. And I'm not going down without a fight.

CHAPTER 17

IZZY

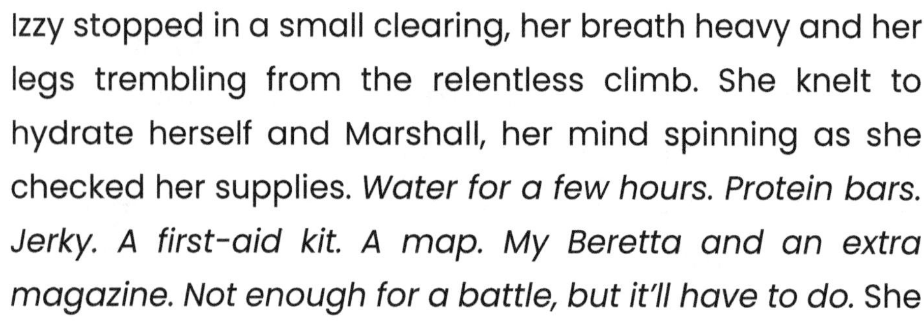

Izzy stopped in a small clearing, her breath heavy and her legs trembling from the relentless climb. She knelt to hydrate herself and Marshall, her mind spinning as she checked her supplies. *Water for a few hours. Protein bars. Jerky. A first-aid kit. A map. My Beretta and an extra magazine. Not enough for a battle, but it'll have to do.* She glanced up at the canopy of trees, their whispering leaves mocking her desperation. *I have a direction but no plan.*

Unfolding the map, she traced her finger across the terrain. *The cabin. I can make it there by evening.* The thought gave her a flicker of hope. Liam's family cabin was well-stocked—hunting rifles, supplies, maybe even the ATVs. She remembered Liam's boasts about the place, how it was maintained but rarely used. Her fingers tightened around the map as her mind shifted. *If the ATVs are running, I could reach Sophie tonight. This could all end tonight.*

Pushing forward, each step felt heavier than the last. The hours passed in a blur of rustling leaves and uneven ground until the cabin's familiar outline appeared over the ridge. For a fleeting moment, its wooden charm was a welcome sight: the tall windows reflecting the sunset, rocking chairs on the porch beckoning her to rest. Then, she saw it. Smoke, curling lazily from the chimney.

Her breath caught, and she ducked behind a tree. *Smoke? Someone's here.* Her heart thundered in her chest as she scanned the surrounding forest. Shadows twisted ominously, each one a potential threat. Then came the crunch of footsteps in the underbrush.

Panic surged through her, and she bolted. *Run. Don't look back.* Marshall kept pace beside her, oblivious to the danger. The footsteps grew louder, closer, and her lungs burned with the effort to outrun them. Her mind raced with images of teeth snapping at her heels. She veered through the trees, dodging branches and leaping over roots until—

A heavy weight slammed into her, driving the air from her lungs. Strong arms wrapped around her, dragging her to the ground. Marshall's barking was frantic, a blur of sound amidst her struggle. A hand clamped over her mouth, stifling her scream.

"Shut up, Izzy!" The voice was harsh, familiar. "It's me! Stop struggling!"

Her body froze. The arms loosened, and she turned, her chest heaving as she stared into the face she thought she'd never see again.

"Liam?" The name fell from her lips, dripping with disbelief and fury. His once-familiar face was nearly unrecognizable—ashen, hollow-eyed, and marred by a gnarled scar running from his brow to his jaw. His clothes hung loosely on his frame, and other, smaller cuts and bruises peppered his skin.

He opened his mouth to speak, but she was already pulling away, her rage igniting.

"How are you alive? What are you—"

"Shh! Get inside!" He cut her off, his grip tightening on her arm as he scanned the forest. "I'll explain, but not out here."

The cabin was just as she remembered—warm, rustic, and stocked with every comfort money could buy. The stone fireplace roared, casting flickering light across the rich wood beams and leather furniture. Marshall wasted no time curling up on the overstuffed couch, but Izzy remained standing, her body rigid with anger and disbelief as Liam crouched by the fire.

His face, illuminated by the flames, looked older, weathered. The scar across his cheek twisted in the shifting light, a harsh reminder of whatever life he'd been living.

"Start talking, Liam." Her voice was sharp, cutting through the crackle of the fire. "How are you alive? What are you doing here?"

He sighed, running a hand through his unkempt hair. "It's complicated, Isabelle…"

"Damnit, Liam! Call me Izzy! Enough with the dramatics and spit it out!" She crossed her arms, her eyes narrowing as she waited for him to stumble through his excuses.

What followed was a tale of selfishness and cowardice, thinly veiled as bad luck. He spoke of drugs, a stolen shipment, a life-or-death debt, and his staged death. The scar, the hiding, the radio silence—it all painted a picture of someone who'd abandoned her and left chaos in his wake.

"And me?" she asked coldly. "Where was I in all this?"

He flinched, his gaze falling to the floor. *Of course. He didn't even think about me.*

"You don't understand—"

"No, Liam. I do. You're the same coward you've always been, taking the easy way out and leaving everyone else to pick up the pieces." Her words landed with precision, and she saw the flicker of shame in his expression. She had little compassion for him or the bed he'd made for himself. At least the scars he now bore would forever remain, reminders of the consequences of his selfishness.

Rage, cold and slicing, lit up his eyes, his twisted expression accompanied by his scar made him look menacing. "Easy?! Nothing about this was easy. I ran for *miles* in the rain, caught whatever ride I could manage along the way, stitched myself up, and survived trying to leave as little trace as possible. It wasn't *easy...*" He paused for a moment, considering what she'd meant. His face sparked with sudden realization, and he looked at her — his eyes falling to her abdomen. "You don't look any different. Are you supposed to be showing by now?" His words were careless and uncaring, mere curiosity.

A piercing pang of grief swept through the hollow hole in her womb at the careless mention of how large that little life may now be, if allowed to continue growing within her. "I..." She swallowed, the lump in her throat growing hard as she attempted to speak. "It was lost. Through no *choice* of my own." The last part, she added with venom, a reminder of their history. A deep frown formed on her face as silver sorrow lined her eyes.

Liam nodded—the first time she'd seen a glimmer of apology cross his features, though the words did not exit his lips. "You've gotta understand, I just couldn't see another way out," his words almost a whisper. His face was drawn with the horror of his circumstances.

"That's always been the problem with you, Liam. You're constantly looking for a way out, instead of *through*." Ignoring him, Izzy moved to the pantry, loading her pack with jerky, water, and anything else useful. She slung the pack over her shoulder and moved to the gun cabinet, selecting a bolt-action rifle and a box of rounds.

"What are you doing?" Liam's voice was sharp, almost panicked.

"Leaving." She didn't look at him as she checked the rifle's chamber. The purpose that spurred her on lay somewhere out there in the wilderness, vulnerable and afraid. She had no time to ponder the actions of craven men.

"Where are you…" He followed her across the living space as she moved to the kitchen, filled her water supply and put a dish on the floor for Marshall.

"What are you doing," Liam demanded, as it occurred to him that Izzy's presence hadn't been for his sake. "You didn't even tell me what the hell you're doing all the way out here on foot."

As Izzy sat in the kitchen chair, she winced as she removed her boots, her feet screaming from the relentless trek. She set to work cleaning and bandaging her blisters, her hands steady despite her exhaustion. Sliding on fresh socks, she flexed her toes gingerly, feeling the tender flesh adjust to the padding. Meanwhile, she recounted the events of the past few weeks to Liam, her tone clinical and detached, mirroring the impersonal way he'd recounted his own story earlier.

She laid it all bare: the eviction notice she'd found taped to her door, the leave of absence from work, the night at the club when everything unraveled, waking in a hospital bed only to learn that Sophie was missing. Her voice remained even, betraying none of the emotional turmoil she carried. Instead, she focused on the facts, as if reducing them to a list might strip them of their weight.

When she finished her feet, Izzy reached for her braid, pulling her hair loose to work through the tangles. She picked out bits of debris—twigs, leaves, the physical remnants of her journey through the wilderness—and started weaving the strands back together. Her hands moved methodically, her eyes fixed on the task as she continued.

"I've been searching for Sophie ever since," she said, her voice steady. "Asking questions, following leads, and piecing together whatever I could. Maggie pointed me toward the shack near the cave." She left out the parts about Gabe—about how his help had carried her this far, about his lies and the sting of betrayal. *He doesn't deserve that part of my story.*

Across the room, Liam's jaw hung slack, the weight of her words sinking in. His face, usually so carefully guarded, was etched with something that looked like regret. "Izzy... I... I don't know what to say."

"Say nothing, Liam. Do nothing. It's what you do best, apparently." Her voice was cold, her stormy blue eyes cutting through him like a blade. She finished lacing her boots, the movements deliberate despite the ache in her feet. Standing, she hoisted her pack onto her shoulders and turned to leave.

As her hand brushed the strap, Liam's hand shot out, gripping her wrist. The sudden contact sent a bolt of anger through her, and her body tensed, her free hand curling into a fist at her side. Her eyes snapped to his, warning him that she wouldn't hesitate to strike if he pushed her further.

But his grip softened, his expression shifting from desperation to something almost tender. "I know I've messed up, Izzy," he said quietly, his voice unsteady. "I know I've been selfish. But you can't go alone. You're... well, you're you."

Her fury flared at the words. *You're you?* Crimson clouded her vision as she yanked her wrist free, taking a step back to put space between them.

"I'm me?!" she spat, her voice rising with the force of her anger. "Where were you, Liam? Where were you when I dealt with every blow by my damn self? Were you hiding here in your little sanctuary, licking your wounds and thinking you'd won?!" Her voice cracked, but her resolve didn't falter.

Liam's eyes dropped, the weight of her words sinking in.

"Don't you dare tell me what I can or can't do." Her voice dropped, low and dangerous, as she pulled the straps of her pack tighter. She took a step toward the door. "Now, give me the keys to the garage. It's the least you can do."

"You can't go alone," he insisted, stepping into her path.

Her eyes burned with fury as she faced him. "I didn't need you then, and I don't need you now – you'd only get in the way." She shoved past him, but his hand on her wrist stopped her.

"Let me help," he said, his voice softer now. "You don't have to do this alone."

She hesitated, her resolve faltering as his words lingered. *Help could mean the difference between finding Sophie and losing her forever.*

"Fine," she said at last. "But if you slow me down, I'll leave you behind. Let's go."

The engines of the ATVs shattered the forest's stillness, their growls bouncing off the towering canopy. Izzy gritted her teeth against the noise, knowing it could give them away but thankful for the speed. Her eyes stayed locked on the winding trail ahead, the ATV's headlights slicing through the oppressive darkness. It had taken too long to find the trail in the night's black maw, the trees seeming to conspire to hide their path. Izzy leaned into the handlebars, her braid snapping behind her like a battle standard. Liam kept close behind, his face pale and set with uncharacteristic determination. Marshall bounded effortlessly alongside, his instincts sharp despite the noise and confusion.

The forest seemed alive, its branches reaching down like skeletal fingers, trying to halt their progress. The trail twisted relentlessly, briars snagging at their clothes and skin, adding to the mounting tension. Izzy's pulse quickened with every mile, her breath shallow and strained. The thought of what lay ahead gnawed at her resolve. She had trained with her rifle, sure—but never against living, breathing humans. The idea chilled her, but her resolve held firm. Sophie needed her. Whatever it took.

Finally, the malformed tree Maggie had described loomed in the faint glow of the headlights. Its grotesque, contorted trunk leaned sharply away from the path to the left, its branches clawing upward as if trying to escape the poisoned ground. Recognition and unease settled over Izzy like a second skin.

"This is it," she murmured, her voice swallowed by the roar of the engines.

They slowed, the ATVs crawling forward as the path narrowed into a dense tangle of underbrush and gnarled roots. Izzy pulled her vehicle to the side and motioned for Liam to do the same. Together, they pushed the machines into the shadows of the trees, covering them with branches. When the engines cut out, silence reclaimed the forest like a jealous lover.

Izzy crouched, her breathing steady but quick as she scanned the woods. The forest felt oppressive, as if the trees themselves were holding their breath. Marshall's ears twitched, his nose to the ground as he sniffed cautiously. Izzy glanced at Liam. To her surprise, he seemed focused, his usual swagger replaced by a grim seriousness. He carried his hunting rifle with an ease she hadn't expected, his pack slung over one shoulder. For the first time, she wondered if maybe he was trying to change.

The trail ahead was claustrophobic, the once-vibrant forest giving way to spindly trees that reached for the sky in desperate solitude. The air grew heavier, colder. Each step forward was like descending into another world—a place where the forest seemed to mourn its own decay. Izzy's gut twisted as they pressed on.

Then she felt it. The cave. The aura was tangible, an oppressive weight in the air that seemed to wrap around her chest like a coiled serpent, tightening with each step. The sulfurous stench hit her nose, sharp and nauseating. She motioned for Liam to stop, crouching low as they reached a rocky outcrop above the cave mouth.

"Stay, Marshall," she whispered, her voice firm but quiet. Marshall whined softly, his eyes locking with hers. She reached down, stroking his head. "Good boy. Stay."

Her heart ached as she left him behind. But it's safer this way.

The overhang offered a clear view of the cave entrance, its dark maw framed by jagged black streaks in the rock, like scars from a long-forgotten battle. A small wooden structure clung to the side of the cave like an afterthought, smoke curling faintly from a chimney. The air here was colder still, the chill sinking into her bones. The stories of the cave played in her mind—the tales of those who entered and never returned.

Izzy swallowed her fear, peering over the ledge. She could hear muffled voices, faint and distorted as they echoed off the wet walls of the cave. She strained her eyes but could only make out the edge of the shack.

"I can't see anything," she murmured to Liam. "Barely the roofline. We need a closer look."

Liam hesitated, his knuckles tightening around his rifle. "You can't go down there, Izzy. They're probably armed, and you have no idea what's waiting for you. You'll get yourself killed."

She sighed, slinging her rifle over her shoulder. "We don't have a choice. No one else is coming, Liam. If we wait too long, Sophie's gone. I couldn't live with that."

Liam ran a hand over his scarred face, his jaw tight. "I'll go."

Izzy blinked, surprised. His voice carried a certainty she hadn't heard from him before. "Liam—"

"No," he cut her off, shaking his head. "I'll go. Just stay here and cover me."

For once, Izzy didn't argue. She watched as Liam adjusted his pack and started down the rocky incline, moving with surprising care. Her chest tightened with every step he took, his figure growing smaller as he neared the edge of the shack. The seconds dragged into eternities, her pulse thrumming in her ears.

Her mind wandered briefly to Gabe, his absence a hollow ache she hadn't expected. Forgiveness wasn't something she gave easily, but for him... she already had. *I was such an idiot.* Her breath hitched. *What if he's not coming?*

The crunch of boots on gravel snapped her back to the present. Liam reappeared, his face pale but composed.

"Two men inside," he said quietly. "Maybe three people crouched on the floor, but I couldn't tell if Sophie's one of them. The guys are armed—didn't see anyone outside."

Izzy nodded, her mind racing. "If we draw them out, we might be able to get inside."

Liam frowned but didn't argue. "You'd better be right."

Her grip on her rifle tightened as the cold from the cave seeped deeper into her skin. She was trembling from more than the cold. "I have to be."

A sharp, clear whistle rang from Izzy's lips as she crouched beneath the low, drooping branches of a thick evergreen, the only greenery that seemed to survive here. The sharp tang of pine hung in the air, grounding her as she hid beneath the natural shield. Muted voices filtered out from the shack, garbled but distinct enough to spike her adrenaline. She cast a glance to her left, spotting Liam crouched low near a large boulder. He was barely visible, but his presence anchored her, a faint reminder that she wasn't entirely alone.

Heart pounding, Izzy braced her rifle against a sturdy branch in front of her, the barrel steady despite the tremor in her fingers. Two men emerged from the shack's lopsided door to investigate the sound, the dim light behind them offering little clarity of the space within. The first man carried a rifle, poised and ready, while the second slung his casually, though his gaze darted around like a predator scanning for prey.

Izzy's breath came in slow, deliberate pulls as she tracked their movements. *Breathe. In. Out.* She fought to quell the panic rising in her chest. These men were armed, and every passing second increased the chance that Liam—or she—would be discovered. Her trigger finger twitched as she wrestled with the morality of her situation. *What if we're wrong? What if Sophie isn't here?* The weight of the decision pressed down on her, suffocating and absolute.

A faint rustling from the woods behind her snapped her focus. She froze, her ears straining to determine whether it was the wind or something far more threatening. The sound grew louder, deliberate, and her stomach clenched as six armed men emerged from the shadows, dressed similarly to the two by the shack.

Izzy's lungs seized as she realized her precarious position. She was trapped—pinned between the men at the shack and the approaching group. Her eyes darted wildly, searching for an escape that didn't exist. Inch by inch, she shifted her weight, willing herself to vanish into the shadows beneath the evergreen's protective branches. *Breathe. In. Out.*

The shouting started before she could think, harsh and guttural commands that reverberated through the trees. The noise was aimed at something barreling through the woods—a blur of white fur streaking toward her. *Marshall.*

Her heart dropped. *No, no, no.* He must have heard her whistle, thinking she'd called for him. His loyalty pierced her like a blade, both a comfort and a curse. Marshall skidded into the clearing, his growls and barks cutting through the chaos. He planted himself in front of her, a white shield against the oncoming storm.

Tears stung her eyes as Izzy broke from her cover, her rifle raised and steady despite the turmoil raging inside her. She rolled into a crouch, spraying pine needles as she landed, and aimed directly at the center man in the group.

The leader sneered at her audacity, his laugh low and menacing. But the laughter died as Izzy chambered a round with a sharp, decisive *clack*. The sound echoed against the cavern walls, and the smirk vanished from his face.

The man furthest to her right twitched, raising his weapon. Instinct took over. Izzy fired, the shot ringing loud enough to silence the forest. The man crumpled, his body hitting the ground with a sickening thud. Blood pooled beneath him, dark and unrelenting, but Izzy couldn't focus on the consequences.

A shout tore through the clearing behind her as the others scattered, the chaos drawing her attention. Movement caught her eye, and she turned in time to see Liam bolting—not toward her, not to help, but up the path they'd descended. *You coward!*

Her momentary distraction cost her. One of the men lunged, but before he could reach her, Marshall intercepted, his teeth sinking into the attacker with a vicious snarl. The man screamed, struggling against the dog's relentless assault.

The sound of a gunshot shattered the air again, and a pained yelp followed. Marshall collapsed to the ground, blood staining his white fur. Struck, Marshall released his grip on the man, leaving nothing but a motionless, mauled pile of flesh.

"No!" Izzy screamed, her voice raw and feral. The sight of her loyal companion lying motionless broke something deep within her. She didn't notice the man closing in until it was too late.

The butt of a rifle slammed into her skull, the force sending her sprawling into the dirt. Stars danced across her vision as pain radiated through her head. She caught one last glimpse of Marshall's still form before the world tilted and went dark.

Her mission failed, spirit finally broken, the red stain of blood against pure white fur a final mocking of all she'd endured.

Unable to face the crushing heaviness of her failure, the darkness beckoned, and she welcomed it.

CHAPTER 18

LIAM

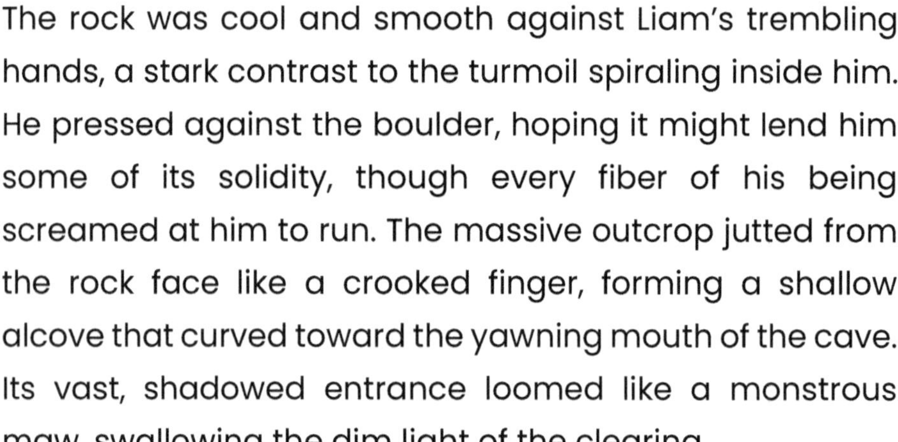

The rock was cool and smooth against Liam's trembling hands, a stark contrast to the turmoil spiraling inside him. He pressed against the boulder, hoping it might lend him some of its solidity, though every fiber of his being screamed at him to run. The massive outcrop jutted from the rock face like a crooked finger, forming a shallow alcove that curved toward the yawning mouth of the cave. Its vast, shadowed entrance loomed like a monstrous maw, swallowing the dim light of the clearing.

He thought of the tales Izzy had recounted about this cursed place, the kind of stories meant to scare children— or, perhaps, fools like him. Those who entered the cave never returned. The forest surrounding it for miles was abandoned, a wasteland of fear and whispered warnings. A shiver danced across his spine, the damp air gnawing at his nerves. He tried to avoid looking into the black depths, but when he did, he swore the darkness shifted, almost as if the cave itself were alive, breathing.

Peering cautiously around the rock, he squinted through the clouded glass of the cabin's single window. The pane was fogged and rotting, but through it, he could make out the faint shapes of two men. Their voices carried faintly into the stillness, casual and unworried. The sound made his skin crawl. These men weren't monsters—they were human. And yet, knowing what they were capable of made them something far worse.

A sharp whistle shattered the eerie quiet, cutting through the air like a knife. Liam flinched, the sound echoing against the cave walls and amplifying into something almost supernatural. His heart slammed against his ribs as he watched the men inside react, their figures moving toward the door. Slowly, cautiously, they emerged into the clearing, rifles at the ready, scanning the trees with practiced efficiency.

Liam held his breath, waiting for them to step further from the cabin. Just a little more. Come on. But they lingered halfway, their eyes sharp and alert, their weapons raised as if anticipating an ambush. The knot in his stomach tightened. They're too close to the cabin. There's no way I can sneak past them without being seen. He glanced toward Izzy's hiding spot among the pines, hoping for some signal, some revised plan. But she remained still, barely a shadow amid the thick foliage.

Then, movement in the trees caught his eye. His breath hitched as he realized what it was—more men. Six of them, armed, advancing from the woods behind Izzy's position. The bile of fear rose in his throat. How did I miss them? The realization slammed into him like a blow. *It's over. We're screwed.*

A white blur darted into the clearing, drawing shouts from the advancing group. His stomach plummeted. Marshall. *That stupid dog! Why didn't she leave him behind?* Liam froze, paralyzed as chaos erupted. The dog barked and snarled, a loyal guardian standing his ground. But Liam knew it was a losing fight.

Then a shot cracked through the night, the sound ricocheting off the cave walls. One of the men in the clearing fell, and Liam's eyes snapped to Izzy, crouched beneath the pine, her rifle trained on her next target. *When did she even get there?* His breath came in shallow gasps, panic clawing at his chest. He tried to move, to act, but his body wouldn't obey.

That's when he saw him—the scarred man in the center of the group. Recognition struck like lightning. *The alley. The knuckle guy.* The tattoos on his neck, the cruel glint in his eye—it was all coming back. *They're connected. All of it.* The drugs. The threats. The missing girls. And now, they'd found him.

Cold dread settled in his bones. If that man saw him, it would be over. He'd finish what he started in that alley. The realization snapped something inside Liam. *I have to get out. Now.*

He turned and bolted, sprinting blindly up the trail they'd come down. His breath burned in his lungs, and every shadow became a hand reaching for him, every branch a claw trying to pull him back. The earth seemed to stretch out farther than he had ever thought possible as a second shot echoed – a distant yelp following. He didn't dare look behind him. If he did, he might have to face the truth of what he was leaving behind.

The ATV came into view, hidden beneath a haphazard cover of branches. His chest heaved as he ripped away the foliage, the vehicle's metallic sheen mocking him in the moonlight. For a moment, his eyes flicked to the second ATV, still untouched. A pang of guilt twisted in his gut, sharp and bitter. But he shoved it down. *She would've gone in without me anyway. She knew the risks.*

His hands shook as he started the engine. The roar of the motor shattered the forest's fragile silence, but he didn't care. *Who cares if you're a hero when you're dead? Better to be alive than be a martyr.*

As he sped away, the headlights cut through the dark, illuminating the twisted limbs of trees that seemed to reach for him, accusing and unforgiving. But he didn't stop. He didn't look back. He couldn't.

After all, dead girls can't tell secrets.

CHAPTER 19

MARSHALL

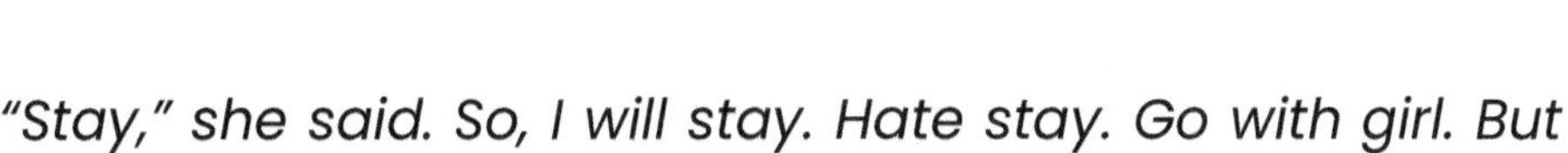

"Stay," she said. So, I will stay. Hate stay. Go with girl. But Marshmallow good boy.

Marshall rose slowly, his paws crunching the brittle earth as he sniffed the ground from his seat on the trail, gathering the hidden truths it carried. Beneath the familiar scents of dirt, pine, and damp leaves, something dark and foul lingered. Something pungent – sulfur stung his nose, mingling with a metallic tang of blood. Fear clung to the air like a ghost, and an ancient, unplaceable wrongness seeped from the shadows. Marshall didn't like it. The fur on his spine stiffened, his entire body standing taut instinctively in warning.

Bad smells. Wrong smells. Fear. Blood. Where is my girl? She went this way. But Marshall, stay?

He shifted uneasily, his loyalty warring with the primal instinct to protect her. Still, her command anchored him. Stay.

Whistle.

The sound echoed through the valley, recognition flooding him as it reached Marshall's ears. A warmth spread through him at the images that clung to that sound, that voice. Messy hair. Warm hugs. The smell of books and blankets. She called, and Marshall answered.

Girl whistles. She needs me. I'm coming! Marshmallow, good boy.

With a gust of speed, Marshall raced down the trail, nose low as he tracked her scent.The ground blurred beneath him as he ran, her unique smell pulling him forward like a beacon. But mingled with it were other odors—strange men, sweat, iron, and cruelty. *Smell is bad. Smell is danger. Must find girl.*

The clearing came into view, and he spotted her crouched beneath a pine tree, her scent laced with fear. His own fear was swept away by his duty, replaced by a primal protectiveness that surged through his veins. He sprinted into the clearing, a white streak against the shadows, barking and growling to draw the danger away.

Girl is here. Bad men too close!

His snarls echoed through the trees as he squared off against the intruders. He bared his teeth, a lion's heart beating in his chest as he stood his ground. Behind him, his girl emerged, rolling from her cover and raising her weapon. Her presence filled him with pride and courage. Together, they faced the danger. Together, they would stand.

Good girl. You are strong. You are brave. I will stay with you.

One of the men laughed, a low, ugly sound that made Marshall's fur bristle. He growled louder, snapping his jaws in warning. The laugh died as Izzy chambered a round, the metallic clack echoing like thunder.

Then came the shot, sharp and deafening. One man fell, his body crumpling to the ground. Marshall barely flinched at the sound, though it rang in his percept hearing – his focus did not waver. *Protect girl. Protect her.* The smell of blood and death filled his nostrils.

But movement from the side caught his eye. Another man lunged for her while her attention was elsewhere. Marshall acted without hesitation, leaping for the attacker with a feral snarl. His jaws found flesh—first the arm, then the leg—and he dragged the man to the ground with unrelenting force. Blood coated his muzzle, its acrid taste driving his determination. Grounded, the panicked man hurled his fist into Marshall, but he was on him again in an instant. This time, to end it.

Hurt my girl, I hurt you.

Another shot rang out, closer this time, followed by a white-hot pain that tore through his side. His body betrayed him, collapsing to the ground as the world tilted. Confusion clouded his senses. *Something wrong. Hurt. Where is girl?*

Izzy's scream shattered the air, raw and desperate. It reached into the depths of Marshall's soul, more painful than any wound. He tried to move, to get up, to fight, but his body wouldn't obey. The forest spun around him, and the scents of blood and gunpowder faded as the men retreated.

Can't protect girl. No.

Marshall's head was heavy as he tried to raise it to look around for his master, his friend. Pain surged through him at the effort. His own breaths became labored, the waves of death lapping at the shore. As the sound of bodies became more distant he feared, but not for death. Not for himself. A defeated whine escaped him.

After a few moments, nothing but the sounds of the woods and the harsh, sharp whispers of the bad men met his ears. The voices and footsteps grew faint. The foul smells became more distant, diluted by the fresh air of the forest as the light wind swept through the sparse trees. His girl's scent went with them.

It's okay, girl. Be safe. Marshmallow loves you.

Marshall's eyes closed, ready to accept the end. The world grew dim, the edges of his vision softening like a dream.

Another smell roused him from his drifting, mingled with the wind, his keen nose piquing his interest, even near death.

Leather. Coffee. Car.

Sad man?

The memory stirred – strong hands, kind voice, scents of soap and metal. Marshall's courage rallied once more, and an urgent whine called Sad Man to him. He tried to lift his head, his tail thumping weakly against the dirt. Rescue. Rescue is here.

Sad man, go save girl.

A warm whisper, "It's okay, Marshall," reached out to grasp him from the grips of death, as a strong calloused hand stroked the fur of his face.

"We'll get them, buddy. We'll get them."

CHAPTER 20

GABRIEL

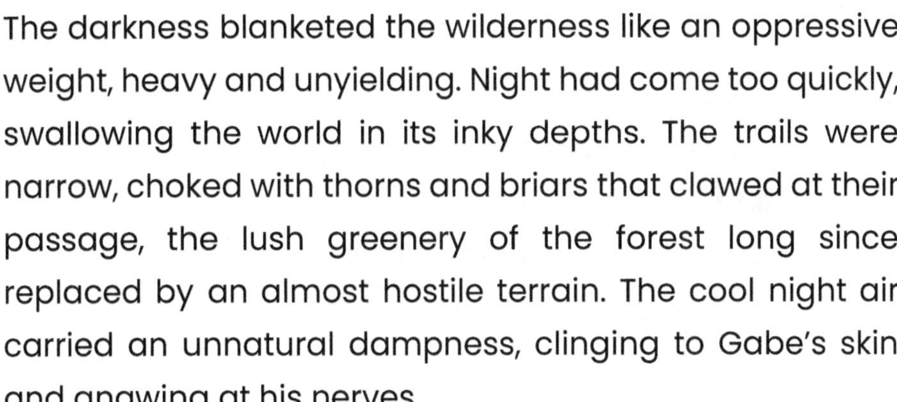

The darkness blanketed the wilderness like an oppressive weight, heavy and unyielding. Night had come too quickly, swallowing the world in its inky depths. The trails were narrow, choked with thorns and briars that clawed at their passage, the lush greenery of the forest long since replaced by an almost hostile terrain. The cool night air carried an unnatural dampness, clinging to Gabe's skin and gnawing at his nerves.

He moved with purpose, his heartbeat steady despite the tension coiling in his chest. The team behind him worked in silence, their precision an echo of his training, but Gabe's focus remained singular: find Izzy.

He followed the signs of recent foot traffic, his mind replaying her message over and over. Coordinates. Directions. Warnings. He could feel her reckless determination pulling him forward. Gabe's jaw tightened.

Izzy, I don't know if I'm gonna kiss you or throttle you when I find you.

As they neared the cave, the atmosphere changed. The air was thick and cloying, as though the earth itself resisted their presence. The rocky terrain rose around them, jagged and foreboding. The faint sound of voices reached his ears, drifting from a dilapidated shack perched at the cave's entrance. Gabe crouched low, signaling the team to spread out.

They moved into position, a silent and calculated force. Gabe's eyes swept the clearing, his night vision highlighting the uneven terrain and the faint outlines of their targets. His breath caught when his gaze fell on a patch of white lying motionless in the dirt.

Marshall.

He moved swiftly, his heart in his throat. The dog's blood-streaked fur glistened in the low light, a dark stain spreading from his side. Two bodies lay nearby, one shot cleanly through the chest, the other's throat mangled beyond recognition. Gabe knelt beside the dog, his hand trembling as he reached out to stroke the loyal animal's face.

"It's okay, Marshall," he whispered, his voice low and steady. "We'll get them, buddy. We'll get them."

Marshall's tail wagged weakly, a feeble thump against the earth. Gabe worked quickly, applying pressure to the wound and wrapping it with practiced efficiency. "You did good, boy," he murmured, his throat tight. "From now on, all the ice cream is yours."

He signaled to the team, his focus narrowing on the shack ahead. The voices inside were louder now, punctuated by the clatter of movement. Gabe's grip on his rifle tightened as he prepared to breach. *This time, we'll be ready.*

As the team moved into position, the memories clawed at him. The living room. Finn's hand on his shoulder. The suffocating weight of failure. His breath hitched, and for a moment, the past threatened to drag him under. He'd tried to suppress the past, the aching guilt that clawed at him, but it hadn't worked. It had eaten away at him from the inside out, like a parasite thriving on his loneliness. It had smothered him, strangled him in his sleep, and visited him in his nightmares.

Please, God. Not now. I need to get to her. Help me.

A steadying force swept through him, like a hand lifting the weight from his shoulders. It wasn't absence; it was presence. It was part of him now—these mistakes, this grief. Not a reminder of his failure, but of his purpose. Finn's loss had left scars, but it had also forged something unbreakable within him.

The blurring in his vision eased, and sweat beaded down his back despite the coolness of the night air. The fog in his mind cleared, and a supernatural stillness washed over him as his breathing deepened and steadied.

Let's finish this.

Gabe signaled, and the team moved as one. The door of the shack burst inward, the entry cleared in seconds. Chaos erupted—shouts, gunfire, the sound of bodies hitting the ground. Gabe's instincts took over, his movements fluid and precise. One man fell to a rifle butt to the chin, another to a series of shots that ended his escape attempt.

Then Gabe saw him: the man from the video. Sandy hair, cocky grin, the man who had led Sophie from the club.

He's mine.

Rage surged through him as he closed the distance, slamming the man onto a table that collapsed beneath the force. The man tried to raise his weapon, but Gabe struck it from his hand with an easy blow. Gabe's fists found their target over and over until the man was motionless. As he stepped away, the man burst across the shards of wood in a desperate reach for his gun. Gabe ended it with a single shot to the head.

Gabe's eyes swept the room for Izzy, finding only a doorway between a falling-down wall and a windowless back room. The back room was worse than he'd imagined. The stench of human suffering hit him like a physical blow. Huddled in the corner were the captives—women, trembling and filthy, their eyes wide with fear. And there, in the center of it all, was Izzy.

Her unconscious form was held by a man, a knife pressed to her throat. Blood trickled from a shallow cut, staining her pale skin. Another wound, a gash in her head was already thickly clotted with blood.

"Come for this, have you?" the man sneered, his voice dripping with malice.

Gabe's rifle was trained between the man's eyes, his finger steady on the trigger. "Get. Your hands. Off her," he growled, his voice low and lethal.

The man smirked, pressing the blade harder – a few droplets of her blood shimmered on the blade. Gabe dropped his weapon, hands raised. "Please," he said, his voice soft but filled with steel. "Let her go."

The man's attention flickered for just a moment. It was all Gabe needed. He surged forward, disarming the man with brutal efficiency –twisting his forearm at an unnatural angle until the knife clanged to the ground. Bones snapped under his grip, and the man screamed in pain. Gabe picked up his rifle, and with a final blow, the man crumpled, unconscious.

His breathing was heavy as he quickly kneeled, cradling Izzy in his arms. *She's safe. Thank you, God.* In the sudden silence, he remembered the group of women present in the room. He looked briefly into each of the trembling faces before him. Recognition flashed. He'd seen some of their pictures a million times as he reminded himself of his purpose, his mission. *The three girls, they're here. Nicole. Amber. Lindsey. With so many others.*

Elation like he'd never known spread through him as he reassured them, "you're safe now. We're gonna get you all out of here." The tone of the chatter from the other room changed, confirming that the men had secured the threat. Gabe was in disbelief for a moment, *we did it. You did it, Izzy.* He reached down to stroke her hair and her face as he gently ran his thumb along her parted lips.

He couldn't help but think of that first night he'd found her. She'd been so beautiful and vulnerable. Helpless. But not this woman before him. Unconscious or no, messy tendrils of hair escaped her blood-matted braid. Mud and blood streaked her face and neck like war paint. The evidence of a hard-fought battle. Far from helpless, this woman emerged from the depths of hell. Refusing to relent. Refusing to back down. From the impossibility of her circumstances. She emerged, scarred but victorious.

Her eyes fluttered open as she winced in pain and looked up at him. After a pause, she smiled—a big, genuine smile that would've brought Gabe to his knees had he not already knelt before her. Relief washed over him, and he couldn't stop the small, breathless laugh that escaped."You're the smartest idiot I've ever met, Izz" he whispered, his voice breaking. Izzy's weak smile was enough to steady him.

Firmly grasping her jaw, he looked into her eyes. "Don't ever do that to me again," he said, his tone a mixture of anger, relief, and something deeper.

She looked at him, then down at his mouth, those stormy eyes seeing everything he hadn't said out loud: his pain, his concern, his apology, and their mutual triumph. She chuckled softly, her eyes sparkling despite the exhaustion. "Noted."

Gabe pressed his forehead to hers, his lips brushing hers in a kiss that said everything he couldn't. When they parted, her gaze moved past him, landing on Sophie.

Sophie was not entirely herself—drug-addled and weighed down by the exhaustion of her captivity. Yet, she was here, breathing and safe. Izzy struggled to sit up, Gabe assisting her with steady hands as she knelt to face her friend.

He waited for Izzy to leap for her, but she sank to her knees, hands on her thighs, and wept at the feet of her friend. All of her worry and turmoil exited her body in those heaving sobs, Gabe resting a hand on her back. He knew the intensity of emotions that followed the rushing streams of adrenaline. Sophie held her. The reunion was quiet, a wordless exchange of relief and gratitude. Silent tears fell from Sophie's eyes, forming trails in the grime that coated her cheeks.

Sophie reached out to Gabe and squeezed his hand in thanks. He gave her a tight-lipped smile in response.

Gabe stood back, letting the weight of the moment sink in. The past no longer haunted him; it propelled him.

They had won.

CHAPTER 21

IZZY

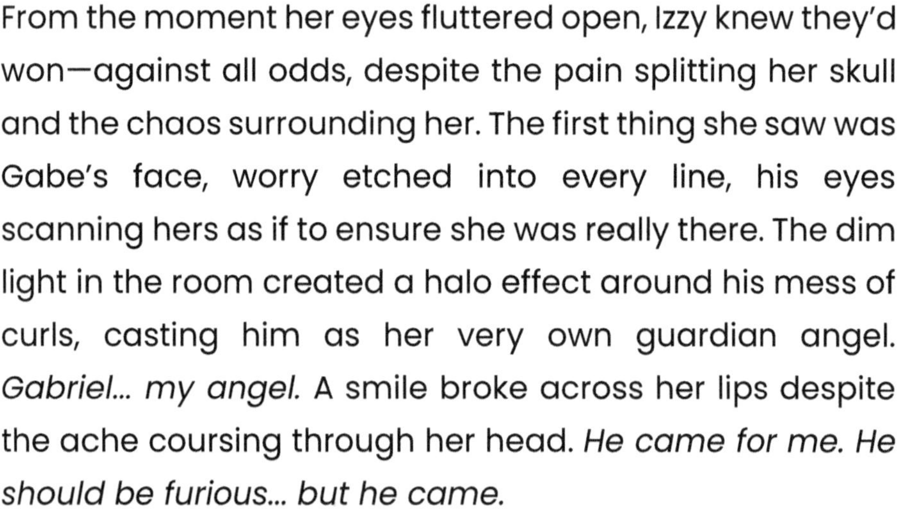

From the moment her eyes fluttered open, Izzy knew they'd won—against all odds, despite the pain splitting her skull and the chaos surrounding her. The first thing she saw was Gabe's face, worry etched into every line, his eyes scanning hers as if to ensure she was really there. The dim light in the room created a halo effect around his mess of curls, casting him as her very own guardian angel. *Gabriel... my angel.* A smile broke across her lips despite the ache coursing through her head. *He came for me. He should be furious... but he came.*

As soon as her smile reached him, Gabe exhaled, the tension in his shoulders easing. "You're the smartest idiot I've ever met, Izz," he said, his own smile tugging at the corners of his mouth.

Izzy tried to laugh but winced as a sharp pain shot through the back of her head. Her hand instinctively went to cradle the tender spot. "That explains the dancing lights," she muttered.

Gabe's hand cupped her jaw, his fingers rough and warm against her skin. The weight of his touch grounded her, sending a small shiver down her spine. "Don't ever do that to me again," he said, his deep voice almost breaking, thick with emotion.

Something inside Izzy cracked open at his words. His concern wasn't hidden behind deflection or gruffness—it was raw, honest, and entirely for her. Tears threatened to spill over, but she focused on his lips instead, the warmth in her chest spreading like wildfire.

She didn't need an apology from him. She understood now, as if the truth had always been etched into his features but hidden beneath her doubt. His secrets, his lies—they weren't meant to hurt her. They were sacrifices, part of the role he'd shouldered to protect the untraceable, to bring people like Sophie home. And she couldn't blame him for that. In his place, she would have burned every bridge, told every lie, to achieve the same end.

He leaned in, and for the first time in as long as she could remember, she didn't flinch, didn't pull back. Instead, she let him close the gap, the walls she'd kept so carefully constructed crumbling away. His lips met hers in a kiss that was tentative but hungry, filled with unspoken promises. She melted into him, her body responding as if it had been waiting for this moment all along.

When they finally broke apart, breathless and flushed, Izzy's thoughts returned to the room, the mission. The smell hit her first—a putrid mixture of sweat, blood, and filth. Turning her head, she saw her.

Sophie.

Her friend was curled in the corner, covered in a blanket, her golden hair matted and streaked with grime. Bruises and scrapes marred her once-bright face, but her green eyes, though dulled with exhaustion, were open. Alive.

Izzy's chest tightened. Relief and sorrow clashed as she studied Sophie, searching her face for the vibrant energy she'd always known. But the spark was gone, snuffed out by whatever horrors she had endured. Their victory sat bitterly on her tongue, knowing the horrors these women faced would remain with them forever.

The tears came without warning. Izzy crumpled, her body shaking as sobs wracked her frame. She wanted to feel victorious, triumphant. But how could she, knowing what

Sophie and the other women had endured? The pain, the terror—it was all there, lingering in the room like a specter.

Sophie moved to her, wrapping Izzy in an embrace. Despite her weakened state, her touch was steady, her presence grounding. "It's okay," Sophie whispered, her voice hoarse but soothing.

Izzy wept harder, clinging to her friend. *She's still here. She's still Sophie.* And though the road ahead would be long and painful, in that moment, the simple fact of her survival was enough.

Gabe had warned her about the scene inside the shack. He'd even offered to shield her eyes. But Izzy refused. She needed to see. Call it sick closure, but she had to know that the men who had done this would no longer walk this earth. At least then, when their faces haunted her dreams, she'd be sure they'd never haunt her waking life again.

Still, even with the warning, she hadn't expected it. She didn't know what to expect. But... this. The addled, aged wooden walls of the front room were a battlefield, speckled and stained with crimson. Holes tore through the timber in so many places that she wondered how much longer the decrepit structure would still stand. Flashlights and the pale moonlight shone through the bullet holes in the front wall, casting eerie shadows over the bodies that lay strewn about the space, Some slumped against walls; others sprawled across the floor in grotesque positions.

Blood pooled on the floor, some smeared with steps and movement – the coppery tang thick in the air. Her gaze landed on the table—or what was left of it. Two shattered legs bore the weight of a man sprawled lifeless across it. His sandy hair was matted with blood, and a gleaming watch on his wrist caught the dim light.

I know him.

Her heart raced as recognition hit. The man who had led Sophie from the club, his arrogance immortalized in that surveillance footage.

But now, there was nothing arrogant about him. His lifeless eyes stared blankly at the broken window, a bullet wound marring his temple. Izzy didn't feel triumph as she'd expected. Only disgust. *If he'd known this was his end, would he have chosen differently?*

Peering through the broken shards, into the night, she could see officers heavily adorned with equipment, as they moved about the clearing.

"Take your time," Gabe said softly from the doorway, his steady presence reassuring her.

Izzy nodded, stepping through the threshold. The cool night air hit her face, washing away some of the heaviness of the shack. She turned to Gabe, her voice barely above a whisper. "What now?"

"Processing," he replied. "The investigation team will be here soon. Lots of paperwork."

As they spoke, Sophie passed by with the other rescued women, wrapped in blankets and being led to the aid station. She smiled faintly at Izzy, who returned it with an exhausted nod, her head throbbing violently.

As if seeing through her, Gabe nodded toward the group offering aid. "You need to get your head looked at, Izz." He looked at her with his head cocked to the side, as if he anticipated a fight on the subject.

"Yeah, probably," she said, her hands going to the sides of her head as if to ease the ache. "I could use some water for right now. Once everyone else has been taken care of, I'll get it looked at."

Izzy's thoughts were scattered with all that had happened, but a sudden flash of realization struck her harder than anything else. *Marshall.* Her head twisted suddenly toward the pine trees where they'd made their stand. "No," her voice a shuddered whisper. Tears filled her eyes, unprepared to give up her companion. She wanted to run in his direction, to find him –

"Don't." Gabe grabbed her arm, turning her around to look at him. "I found him, Izz. He's okay."

A relieved sob gripped her as her chest rose, hitting her like a wave. Following Gabe's lead, she found her loyal companion bundled in blankets, his tail wagging weakly at her approach. He lay next to a tall stick acting as an IV pole, a bag of fluid trailing a plastic line somewhere under the blanket. She dropped to the ground beside him, cradling his face as tears streamed down her cheeks. They lay almost nose to nose as Izzy stroked his face softly, overcome by the depth of her gratitude. He licked her tears and lay his head down to bask in her praise. Gently, she lifted the blanket to see a bandage tightly wrapped around his middle, a small spot soaked through with blood.

"You're the best boy, Marshmallow," she whispered. "My best boy."

Gabe stood guard, watching them interact, a lightness in his brown eyes that she hadn't seen before. *Maybe it's the moonlight.* "I don't know a lot about dogs, but he had lost a lot of blood when I found him. I bandaged him up the best I could. O'Neal was the one whose sister is a vet." Gabe nodded his thanks to a handsome dark-haired man behind the aid station, who held up a hand in greeting. "He seems to have perked up a bit since we went in," he finished.

Tears traced a path across Izzy's nose and dripped steadily onto the dirt beneath her. Her voice wavered, thick with emotion. "Thank you, Gabe. For everything." She couldn't meet his gaze without the threat of breaking entirely, so she kept her eyes down, focusing on the ground.

"No, thank you, Izzy," Gabe replied softly, his tone serious.

The unexpected response made her look up, confusion knitting her brows together. "Me?" she asked, incredulous, her voice barely above a whisper.

Gabe narrowed his eyes slightly, his expression unreadable as he crouched down to meet her gaze. "You really think we just came in to save the day?" He gestured broadly toward the men around them, his lips tugging into a wry smirk.

Izzy followed his gesture, taking in the sight of the officers, the aftermath of the battle, and the women being cared for by the aid team. She cocked her head, her confusion deepening. "I mean… yeah, you kind of did," she said, matter-of-factly.

He shook his head, a small huff of disbelief escaping him. Lowering his gaze, he studied his hands for a moment before looking back at her, his eyes brimming with sincerity. "We never would have found any of them if not for you, Izzy. This was my mission for months—those girls… I've been searching for so long." His voice cracked, the weight of all the time and effort poured into the search evident. "We all have. And until you showed up, we didn't have anything. No leads, no hope. You did that. So, yes, thank you, Izzy."

The words settled over her like a warm blanket, stirring a tingle of pride deep in her chest. It wasn't arrogance, but a quiet gratitude that her pain and persistence had meant something—that Sophie's suffering hadn't been in vain. She lowered her gaze, her cheeks flushing, unsure how to respond to such heartfelt praise.

But Gabe wasn't finished. He tilted her chin up with gentle fingers, his touch firm but reverent. Their eyes locked, and Izzy felt her breath hitch in her throat.

"I didn't do the saving tonight, Izz," he murmured, his voice low and unwavering. "So don't you dare dismiss what you did." Leaning in closer, his large hand cradled the side of her neck, his thumb brushing away the grime on her cheek in a tender stroke. "You saved me, Isabelle. In every way that matters."

Her heart stuttered at the sound of her name on his lips, spoken with such warmth and meaning. She decided then and there that she liked the way he said it, the way it made her feel seen, whole.

Tilting her face toward him, Gabe kissed her. This time, there was no hesitation, no uncertainty. His lips were firm and insistent, sending a bolt of electricity straight through her. The coolness of the forest air contrasted sharply with the heat radiating between them as he held her close, as though he couldn't bear the thought of letting her go.

His kisses weren't frantic but deliberate, savoring every second, every inch of her lips. They explored her softly yet thoroughly, as if he were committing her to memory. Izzy's hands found their way to his chest, curling into the fabric of his shirt as she kissed him back with equal fervor.

When they finally broke apart, breathless and flushed, Izzy's thoughts were no longer clouded by the chaos of the night. Instead, a newfound clarity washed over her.

In the moonlit clearing, surrounded by the echoes of the past few hours, she realized that help wasn't what she'd truly needed all this time. It was this—this raw, unfiltered connection. To be wanted. To be needed so deeply that help arrived without her having to ask, without her having to earn it.

Forgiveness, trust, healing—all of it would come in time. For now, it was enough to know that this beautifully flawed man had chosen her. And she was ready to trust him with everything.

Izzy nestled between Gabe's legs, her head resting against his chest. The steady rhythm of his heartbeat was a comforting anchor in the chaos they'd just endured. A thick bandage wrapped across her forehead bunched her already messy hair into awkward directions. If she caught sight of her reflection, she was sure she'd be appalled. It made her strangely thankful for all the shattered glass around her— no mirrors to remind her of the disheveled mess she must be.

She'd nodded off a few times, exhaustion pulling her into brief, restless naps. Gabe held her upright every time, his arms steady around her as though he feared she might slip away if he let go. Despite the soreness in her body and the pounding in her head, she felt... content.

Nearby, Sophie lay curled into a tight ball beneath a blanket, her thin frame barely moving as she slept. She'd tucked herself close to Marshall's side, his massive body acting as a living heater. Izzy couldn't help but smile softly at the sight. Even in his injured state, Marshall managed a slight wag of his tail in his sleep, the corners of his mouth turned up in what looked like a dog's version of a grin.

The peace was interrupted by the echo of shouting voices emerging from the woods. Both she and Gabe sat up, alert as officers pushed two men forward into the clearing, their arms shackled behind them.

One of the men thrashed wildly, his curses and demands cutting through the morning air. "I have names! I want a plea deal! I'm not going down for this!" he yelled, his voice grating and panicked. A string of colorful curses followed, raising Izzy's eyebrows at the sheer creativity.

The other man was smaller but muscular, his silence more unnerving than his companion's outburst. His face was battered, blood trailing from his nostrils, and his crooked nose bore evidence of a fresh break. As the group drew closer, dawn began to chase away the heavy shadows of the night, soft light illuminating every detail.

Izzy's stomach churned as her eyes landed on the larger man. Bald, with dark tattoos crawling up his neck and a jagged scar cutting across his eyebrow, he was a carbon copy of a memory she wished she could erase. *I wonder where he ran off to.*

"Ah. A squealer. We love those," Gabe muttered with a smirk, his tone dripping with dry humor. He nodded toward the officer restraining the larger man, who returned the gesture with a subtle nod of acknowledgment. Izzy marveled at the unspoken language shared between them—a shorthand born from trust and experience.

But her thoughts drifted elsewhere. Watching the scarred man struggle against his captors made her stomach twist with that familiar memory, one far closer to home. Liam. A wound of betrayal reopened, raw and festering, as her mind conjured images of him lounging comfortably in his parents' cabin, sipping whiskey by a roaring fire, safe and far from harm. Her blood simmered at the thought.

"That reminds me," Izzy said, her voice laced with bitterness as she turned to Gabe. "Do you remember how I told you about my ex? The one in the car accident?"

Gabe's brows furrowed as he looked at her, curiosity flickering in his dark eyes. "Yeah... what reminds you?"

Izzy let out a humorless laugh, shaking her head as she stared at the shackled men. "This. All of it."

For the first time, she didn't hold back. The words came tumbling out—raw, unfiltered, and cathartic. She told him everything: the parties, the betrayal, the crash, the lies Liam spun to save himself while leaving her to pick up the pieces. She spoke of the anger that had simmered within her ever since and the hollow ache of being abandoned when she'd needed him most.

And as the story poured out of her, she realized she wasn't just telling Gabe. She was finally letting it go.

CHAPTER 22

GABRIEL

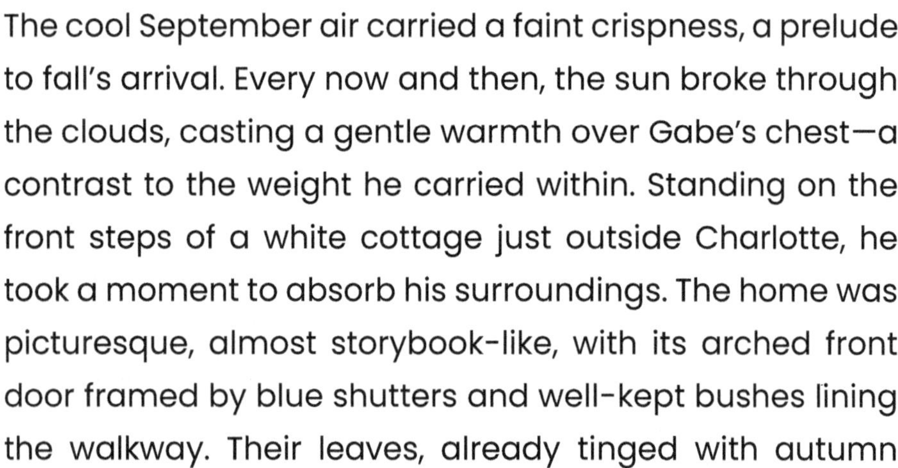

The cool September air carried a faint crispness, a prelude to fall's arrival. Every now and then, the sun broke through the clouds, casting a gentle warmth over Gabe's chest—a contrast to the weight he carried within. Standing on the front steps of a white cottage just outside Charlotte, he took a moment to absorb his surroundings. The home was picturesque, almost storybook-like, with its arched front door framed by blue shutters and well-kept bushes lining the walkway. Their leaves, already tinged with autumn hues, looked ablaze in the fleeting sunlight.

Through the large front windows, he caught a glimpse of the Carter family. They were huddled together in the living room where he and Jenkins had just delivered their update. The room was as bright and pristine as a blank canvas—a clean slate, he hoped, for their lives moving forward. The embrace he saw was bittersweet, the warmth of their unity overshadowed by the pain that had led them to this moment.

The cottage belonged to Nicole Carter, one of the women they'd rescued. At just twenty-one years old, she was a university student with dreams interrupted by a nightmare she hadn't chosen. Gabe couldn't shake the details she had shared during her initial interview with detectives. Her voice trembled as she recounted that summer day on the lake—how carefree it had been, filled with laughter and the thrill of new friendships formed with another group of young boaters.

One man, in particular, had charmed her. He'd introduced himself as John, and as Nicole described his dark blonde hair and polished appearance, Gabe's gut tightened. *The same sandy-haired bastard.* The thought burned through him.

Nicole had gone on to explain how she and her friends didn't hesitate to meet the group for drinks later that evening. But her memory of the night dissolved into flashes—blurry images of a bar, fragmented moments of disorientation. The next thing she remembered was the jarring sensation of an off-road vehicle, the engine roaring as it tore through the woods.

Horror and relief intertwined when she revealed that her two friends, Amber and Lindsey, had also been taken. They had survived captivity together, though the shared trauma had forged a bond none of them would have chosen.

Her recounting of the shack was gut-wrenching. Every detail—every indignity, every instance of suffering—hit Gabe like a physical blow. He'd heard stories like this before, in training, during debriefs, but nothing prepared him for the rawness of hearing it from someone who had lived it. He felt a hollow ache imagining what Nicole must endure in her nightmares, the lasting scars her captors had left on her body and mind. Even after being freed, the torment hadn't ended. She described the agony of withdrawal, her body still clawing its way back to normalcy after weeks of being drugged.

Rescued, yes. But whole? That would take much longer, if it was even possible.

Gabe exhaled slowly, forcing the tension in his chest to subside. This visit was only one stop on a list he'd insisted on completing himself. No one had asked him to make these visits, to sit face-to-face with the survivors and their families, but he needed to. There was nothing he could say to erase what had happened, but maybe he could offer a sliver of peace. Closure. And maybe, in doing so, he could start mending the fractured pieces inside himself.

As he climbed into the passenger seat of the vehicle, Jenkins glanced at him, sunlight splayed across his dark skin through the windshield. "Where to next?"

Gabe glanced down at the padfolio in his lap, its pages filled with names, dates, and addresses. Last on the list was Lucia Martinez. Twenty-two. She'd spent her birthday in captivity. The weight of her name pressed down on him—one they hadn't even linked to the case until her rescue.

"She wasn't even on our radar," Gabe muttered, more to himself than Jenkins. His stomach twisted as he considered the implications. Lucia had been a name on an entirely separate missing persons list, her case unconnected to the string of abductions they'd been investigating.

How many leads had they overlooked? How many women had been lost because the pieces hadn't fit together in time?

Jenkins didn't respond, but his silence was grounding. Gabe knew the questions were dangerous—pointless spirals into *what if* scenarios that would only weigh him down. The women were safe now. They'd found them. And while the path had been circuitous and fraught with obstacles, they'd gotten here. For that, he was grateful.

Still, as the vehicle pulled away from the idyllic white cottage, Gabe couldn't shake the gnawing feeling that there was more work to be done. Scars, after all, didn't fade overnight.

Jenkins chatted amiably during the short drive, and Gabe responded with the kind of effortless banter that came from shared experience. Despite everything, he was grateful for his partnership—a steady presence he could rely on. Jenkins wasn't Finn, and maybe no one ever would be. That kind of bond wasn't easily replaced. But Jenkins had his six, and for now, that was enough.

The events after the cabin raid had unfolded quickly. Gabe and Jenkins had been called into the Chief's office just days later. Their teamwork during the operation hadn't gone unnoticed, and the Chief, with his signature mix of gruffness and pride, had recommended their transfer to the Special Investigations Unit. The opportunity had felt more like an order than a suggestion, but Gabe didn't mind.

He'd spent part of the meeting talking about Izzy—how instrumental she'd been in cracking the case. Gabe's voice had brimmed with genuine admiration as he described her investigative instincts and grit. He even mentioned her new role at Blue Horizons Media, where she'd taken a position in the Investigative Reporting Unit. Gabe had gone on for so long that Jenkins had leaned back in his chair, smirking with quiet amusement as if to say, *Alright, we get it.*

Despite Gabe's enthusiastic detour, the Chief had remained focused on the matter at hand. The transfer came with more training and exams, but both detectives were eager for the challenge. For Gabe, it wasn't just a career move. It felt like a continuation of something he'd started long ago—a chance to do good in Finn's memory. It reminded him of his childhood obsession with Sherlock Holmes, the endless hours spent devouring mysteries. Becoming a detective had always been in the cards, even if the path had been steep and winding.

As the Chief shook their hands, he had added with a knowing smile, "I'll vet Ms. Reed for a liaison position with the department. But, Walsh... it's rare for you to speak so highly of someone. Makes me wonder if there's more to the story." The Chief's raised eyebrow and conspiratorial wink toward Jenkins had left Gabe tight-lipped, though his smirk betrayed him. *The Chief still doesn't miss a thing.*

Pulling up to the Martinez home, Gabe took in the quiet neighborhood. Tree-lined streets framed the modest houses, their yards dotted with autumn's first fallen leaves. Lucia's home radiated warmth—a brick exterior softened by vibrant landscaping and a small front porch adorned with a swing and potted plants.

Gabe knocked, the sound echoing softly in the stillness. When the door opened, a bearded man stood before him, his posture tense and his dark eyes wary. Gabe took in the man's broad shoulders and weathered hands, the kind of strength earned through hard work. He understood the guarded demeanor; this was a father who had endured unimaginable loss and barely clawed his way back to normalcy.

"Mr. Martinez?" Gabe asked, his tone careful.

"Yes. How can I help you?" The words were polite, but the edge in his voice was impossible to miss.

"I'm Detective Walsh, and this is Detective Jenkins. We're here to discuss some updates in Lucia's case." Even after so many of these house calls, Gabe still felt unnatural announcing himself with his new title: *Detective*. It felt odd on his lips. He fidgeted with his tie as he waited for the man's response. *And I'm not sure I'll ever get used to wearing a suit.*

Mr. Martinez hesitated before stepping aside to let them in. The interior of the home mirrored its exterior: cozy and welcoming, with warm wood tones and an abundance of greenery. Plants hung from macramé holders, their vines trailing gracefully, while others bloomed on shelves and tabletops. A woman with kind eyes turned from the kitchen sink, her hands still wet. After a quiet exchange with her husband, she greeted the detectives warmly and called down the hall, "Lucia!"

When Lucia appeared, Gabe's heart clenched. The girl who emerged looked fragile, her white sundress skimming her thin frame as she moved toward them. Her eyes, once full of life, now seemed hollow, her steps slow and deliberate as if a great weight pressed on her. Even in her own home, the past lingered—the ghost of herself, walking through life.

"Lucia, I don't know if you remember me. I'm Gabriel Wal—
"

"I remember you." Her voice was flat, void of emotion, and it took all of Gabe's strength to keep his expression neutral. He nodded and followed as the woman led them into the sitting room, where they settled onto a plush sofa. Thin white curtains billowed in the breeze. Rays of sunlight poured through the open windows kissing the leaves of even more greenery that adorned the space.

"All of your plants are very beautiful, Mrs. Martinez. You clearly have a green thumb," Gabe complimented in an attempt to break the ice.

The woman smiled sadly. "It's my Lucia that has the green thumb. Her garden and plants used to bring her such joy, so I've been picking them up everywhere since..." She lowered her eyes and busied her hands by fixing her hair, unable to finish. A mother – trying desperately to heal what only time can soften. *How helpless she must feel.* She swallowed, and Gabriel nodded, allowing the silence to finish the conversation.

Gabe found that the hardest part of these conversations was reopening the wounds these people were trying to heal or forget. He found it easiest to start with the facts, and take it smooth and steady. *Like Finn would have.*

"Let me get straight to the point, then. There's been a development in the case. One of the captors, during his interviews, negotiated a plea deal in exchange for a series of names of those involved. As it stands, this organization went much further than kidnapping women. They were also smuggling a variety of drugs all over the country in very high quantities. It explains why they had so many drugs accessible to them to sedate the girls." He looked at Lucia, hoping to be sensitive to her reactions.

Her face remained unreadable, her gaze distant. So, he continued. "Last Thursday, twenty men were arrested on various charges and are being held in custody. After being notified that their names were provided to us by their previous colleague, all of them have agreed to plead guilty to charges in some form or another."

When he finished, Lucia simply asked, "Is there anything else?"

Anything else?! This is huge!

Her detachment struck him. Gabe cleared his throat, reminding himself that this wasn't about him. He wanted her to feel something—relief, anger, anything—but everyone copes differently. "No," he replied quietly. "No, that's it. The department wanted the families to hear about the arrests before the media made it public."

He hung his head, looking down at his padfolio to divert his attention from those sad, empty eyes. They reminded him of the cave mouth, yawning open to suck in the life around it.

"Thank you, Detective." Lucia rose from the sitting area, and when Gabe thought she would leave the room, she sat before him on the coffee table. She faced the open window, eyes closed as she breathed in the breeze. After a long pause, Lucia leaned forward, her fingers brushing the petals of a lily on the coffee table.

Her voice, barely above a whisper, carried the weight of her pain. "I remember the night you came for us. When you came running into that back room..." Her lower lip trembled as she took a shuddering breath. "I was one of the first to arrive there. I and another girl, Alyssa, were taken only days apart... I don't know that I'll ever forget a lot of what happened in that place..."

Pausing, her dark eyes found his again, this time brimming with tears. "But I will *never* forget your face, Mr. Walsh." Her gaze bore into him, as if his every feature were etched into her memory. "Thank you..." she said softly, "for never giving up on us."

Unable to handle the rising tide of emotion threatening to engulf him, Gabe swallowed hard and nodded softly. Jenkins knowingly placed a hand on his partner's shoulder, and they rose to leave.

Later, Gabriel sat behind the wheel, sipping his lukewarm coffee, and staring out the windshield. His hands rose to wipe his face and eyes, hoping to clear away some of the emotional tangle that had settled within him during the day. *What a rollercoaster.*

Jenkins reclined his head against the headrest, "Long day," he drawled.

Gabe chuckled, the sound low and tired. "Yeah."

"What's next?"

Gabe glanced at the clock on the dash. Almost 3:00 PM— quitting time for once. It struck him as odd, the concept of clocking *out*. So many months spent consumed by his work. It felt strange. It felt good.

His mind wandered to a certain dog and the woman who owned him. "Ice cream and a beach date," he said with a wide grin.

Jenkins smirked, gently punching his shoulder. "Whipped."

Gabe didn't argue. As he drove, he thought only of Izzy, and his blood hummed at the thought of her warm lips against his. No matter how hard he tried, he couldn't wipe the silly smile from his face. *Yeah, I'm whipped alright.*

CHAPTER 23

IZZY

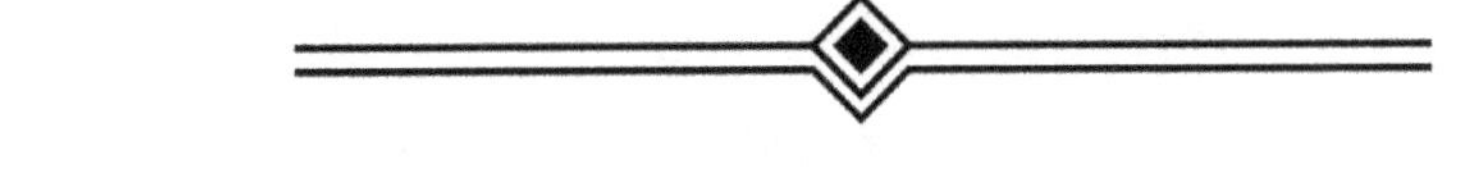

The waves rolled in, crashing on the shore in a steady, rhythmic parade. Izzy had found a secluded stretch of beach, the perfect place to gather her thoughts and write. The sand was warm beneath her bare feet, still holding the sun's heat despite the cooling breeze rolling in from the water. Behind her, a towering sand dune formed a natural recline, its gentle slope shielding her from the world beyond. Above, a cluster of palm trees swayed lazily in the wind, their leaves whispering secrets to the sky.

Marshall frolicked in the shallows, snapping at the tips of waves as they broke against the shore. His thick fur clung to him, heavy with saltwater, and every so often, he'd pause to shake himself off, sending a sparkling spray in all directions. Izzy smiled, marveling at his boundless joy. It had been too long since she'd been here, by the sea, allowing the endless horizon to remind her of her smallness.

The vastness of nature always left her awestruck. The powerful wild of the mountains, the unstoppable might of the ocean—it was humbling, but not in a way that diminished her. Rather, it offered perspective. Somewhere beyond this beach, the world was filled with pain and cruelty, but here, the waves continued, unbothered by the chaos. The juxtaposition felt both cruel and beautiful. Maybe it was both.

With her laptop balanced on her knees, Izzy's fingers moved steadily over the keys. She was drafting her story—*their* story. It was hard to know where to begin. So much had happened in such a short time, and each memory carried its own weight.

Only days after that long, harrowing night in the woods, the public began demanding answers. The sheer scale of the police presence—helicopters, SWAT vehicles, unmarked cars—had not gone unnoticed. When the first press release announced the dismantling of a major trafficking ring, the story exploded. Within hours, details about the operation's connection to drug smuggling emerged, adding fuel to the fire.

Izzy hadn't expected her name to be released in the flurry of media coverage, but it was, linking her directly to the search efforts. Her phone lit up almost immediately with a call from Janice, her boss at *Blue Horizons.*

Janice's voice wavered between awe and disbelief, peppering the conversation with awkward platitudes like, "I'm so glad you're okay," and "I just can't believe it." Izzy had offered as much as she could without violating the ongoing investigation's restrictions. Before the call ended, Janice insisted Izzy speak to the head of the Investigative Reporting Unit.

Izzy had dreamed of a break like this for years, but when the opportunity finally came, it felt different than she'd imagined. Sitting across from the unit head in a sleek office overlooking the city, she felt a surprising sense of detachment. The excitement she'd expected—the kind that would leave her buzzing with energy—was dulled. Maybe it was exhaustion. Maybe it was the weight of everything she'd experienced. *Nothing like a near-death experience to offer some healthy perspective.*

The pitch was straightforward: once the investigation concluded, they wanted Izzy to write an insider's account of the trafficking ring. Her firsthand experience gave her a perspective no other journalist could provide. She agreed, but with conditions.

"This isn't going to be about me," she said firmly, holding the editor's gaze. "If I write this story, it has to be about the women. About Sophie. About all the others. It has to expose the evil hiding in plain sight."

The editor nodded, clearly impressed by her conviction, but Izzy wasn't done. "And it can't be sanitized. People need to understand the danger. The fear. The helplessness. I don't want to glorify myself or make it seem like everything worked out neatly. It didn't. Those women have scars that won't ever fully heal."

Izzy had no illusions about the reach of her words. Evil this pervasive couldn't be eradicated with one article, no matter how powerful. But she believed in the power of refusal—refusing to look away, refusing to stay silent, refusing to let this sickness thrive in the shadows.

She accepted the assignment, not for the byline or the recognition, but for the chance to make people care. To make them act.

Back on the beach, Izzy paused her typing and gazed out at the horizon. The sky and sea met in a hazy blur, infinite and unknowable. The breeze carried the faint tang of salt, and the sound of Marshall's playful splashes brought a soft smile to her face.

This was why she fought. For moments like this—for beauty, joy, and freedom. For the chance to choose her own story.

And for Sophie, who deserved to find her own peace beneath a sky this endless.

From behind her, Izzy heard the soft crunch of shifting sands. The wind pulled strands of hair loose from her ponytail, whipping them across her face, and she smiled, knowing exactly who was approaching. Marshall barked excitedly, bounding toward their guest with a tail wagging so hard it looked like it might propel him off the ground.

Izzy's heart quickened, a thrill rushing through her at the thought of being near Gabe again. She hadn't expected this—a contentment so deep it felt like home. As he rounded the corner, she almost laughed with sheer joy. His curly hair was tousled by the ocean breeze, sunglasses perched casually on his nose. His white shirt was unbuttoned, revealing a broad chest, and the rolled-up sleeves exposed the strong lines of his tattooed forearms. Barefoot, with his suit pants cuffed to his calves, he held up a bag in greeting, his grin as easy and magnetic as ever.

Marshall reached him first, nearly knocking him over in his enthusiasm. Gabe laughed, steadying himself as he rubbed the dog's sides with both hands. "Take it easy, Marshmallow man," he said, crouching to inspect Marshall's healing wound. His touch was gentle as he checked the scabs, murmuring something to the dog that only they could understand. Izzy's heart swelled, her chest warm with the simple joy of watching the two of them together.

Gabe stood, his voice deep and a little rough from the drive. "Long trip, but this view makes it worth it."

Izzy turned to the waves, their rhythmic crashing both powerful and peaceful. "Yeah, it's beautiful here. It's been ages since I've been to the beach."

Gabe stepped closer, towering over her as he sat beside her. He reached out, brushing a loose strand of hair from her face. His gaze was warm, but there was a spark of mischief in his eyes. "I wasn't talking about the beach, Izz."

Her breath hitched, and her cheeks flushed. Forget butterflies; it felt as though a whole flock of seagulls had taken flight in her stomach. She looked down, biting her lip as a smile spread across her face. Gabe cupped her chin with both hands, tilting her head up to meet him. The kiss he gave her was deep and wanting, his lips coaxing hers open. Strong hands tangled in her salt-tousled hair as he pulled her closer, leaning back against the dune. His arms wrapped around her, and she let herself sink into him, utterly at peace.

Later, eating their ice cream, they reclined in each other's arms. Gabe reached over occasionally to spoon Marshall some of his very own pint of Peanut Butter Explosion, as promised. Between bites, they laughed together as Marshall deadpan stared at them until the next bite arrived in his drooling maw. Between laughter and the cool sweetness of the ice cream, Izzy's spirit felt light, as if it might take flight with the ocean breeze.

The next day, Gabe had insisted on taking her to the mountains to see the autumn leaves. After dropping Sophie off for brunch with her family, they hit the road with Marshall happily sticking his head out the back window.

Sophie had been doing better. Each day, her haunted look softened, replaced by quiet determination. Izzy admired her friend's strength, the way she intentionally sought joy in small moments. When Sophie withdrew, Izzy didn't press. She simply stayed close, a silent comfort when words couldn't help. In those moments, Izzy realized that their bond had deepened through their shared pain. There were no more walls between them, no secrets left to hide.

With the windows down and the crisp air whipping through her fingers, Izzy leaned back, savoring the moment. The trees, ablaze with fiery reds and oranges, blurred as they sped down the highway.

Ahead, a sign warned: *LITTER CREW AHEAD*. Gabe slowed the car, and as they approached, a group of men in orange jumpsuits came into view, collecting trash along the roadside.

Izzy froze, then grinned. No way.

There he was—Liam. The thick scar down his face was unmistakable, his once-pristine arrogance now reduced to a lazy shuffle as he poked at garbage with a stick. Orange is not your color, Liam.

She leaned over Gabe and honked the horn. Liam turned, his scowl deepening as she waved grandly, her smile radiant and victorious.

Sitting back, Izzy couldn't help the smug satisfaction that spread through her. A few weeks earlier, she'd received a call from Liam's parents. They'd begged her to sign a non-disclosure agreement in exchange for paying her rent indefinitely. Apparently, Liam had returned home only to be promptly arrested. Charges ranged from DUI and fleeing an accident to a drug trafficking connection tied to his bald, tattooed associate.

Izzy had considered the deal, especially with her eviction looming, but the terms didn't sit right. Especially after learning that Liam's lawyers were able to negotiate his sentence down to 20 days in jail and a long stint of community service. So instead, she'd mailed the NDA back, ripped to shreds, with a note reminding them of Liam's breach of contract on his rental – since he was alive and everything. The resulting check for her back rent had been sweet, but not as satisfying as knowing she'd be free to tell the truth.

Now, as she watched Liam shuffle along the roadside, she couldn't stop smiling. *Sometimes, life really does come full circle.*

As Izzy stepped into the restaurant, the gentle glow of dangling lights above cast warm halos, reflecting off the polished wood floors. Their soft radiance seemed to dance in her eyes, drawing Gabe's gaze toward her as he held the door open. His hand lingered on her back, a silent, steadying presence that guided her through the threshold.

Her breath caught as her eyes landed on a long table near the center of the room. The booth on one side was plush with leather, while chairs with dark wooden frames lined the other. Seated there, her family—both by blood and by the bonds of shared trials—filled the space with a comforting hum of laughter and conversation.

Her father's warm grin met her instantly, his eyes twinkling with pride. He raised a hand in greeting, a silent message: *I'm glad you're here.* Across from him sat Sophie, her blonde hair catching the light as she waved excitedly. Sophie's smile was radiant, a quiet testament to her resilience. Beside her sat Officer Carter O'Neal, his broad shoulders and easy-going demeanor radiating an infectious energy.

Izzy stifled a grin as she remembered Gabe's story about introducing them. He'd done it on a whim, but it had been the perfect match. Despite O'Neal's playful nature, Gabe swore he was one of the most steadfast and protective men he knew. "She needs someone like that," he'd told Izzy, his voice laced with brotherly concern. Naturally, Gabe had already delivered a stern warning to O'Neal about breaking Sophie's heart.

"Of course, you did," Izzy had teased, her voice full of affection.

As they approached the table, Izzy's heart swelled. This was what safety looked like. Not a place, but people—those who fought for you, stood beside you, and helped you find your footing when the ground beneath you felt unsteady.

Yet, as she exchanged smiles with Sophie and her father, a shadow of thought passed through her mind. The other women. The ones who had been rescued from the cabin.

Were they safe?

Had they found their own family, their own Gabe or Sophie, to anchor them?

Did they wear their scars with pride, or did they carry them in the hidden hours of the night, where no one could see their pain?

Izzy prayed for them often, sometimes in moments like these when her own joy felt almost too much to bear. She hoped their nights were no longer haunted and that their days brought glimpses of a brighter future. Her gaze softened as she resolved to check in on them, even if it was just through a letter or call.

Gabe's voice broke through her thoughts as he leaned down to murmur in her ear, "You okay?"

His hand, still resting on her back, brought her back to the present. She tilted her head up to meet his gaze and smiled softly. "Yeah. Just... thinking about how blessed we are."

He nodded, his own eyes reflecting a depth of understanding that needed no words. "We are," he agreed, guiding her to the table.

As they reached the table, her father rose from his seat, wrapping her in a firm, familiar embrace. "There's my girl," he said, his voice rough with emotion.

"Hi, Dad," she said, squeezing him back. She felt his strength, his steadiness, and for a moment, she was the little girl he used to carry on his shoulders, pointing out the stars.

Sophie greeted her next, pulling her into a hug that was both light and grounding. "You look amazing," Sophie said, her green eyes bright.

"You do too," Izzy replied, meaning it. The sparkle in Sophie's eyes had returned, like sunlight breaking through clouds.

O'Neal stood next, extending a hand to Gabe before turning to Izzy with an exaggerated bow. "Miss Reed, an honor," he said, his voice playful.

Izzy rolled her eyes with a laugh. "Carter, you're insufferable."

"True," he replied, unbothered, as Sophie smacked his arm lightly.

As the group settled, the conversation flowed easily. Gabe slid into the booth beside Izzy, their knees brushing beneath the table. His presence was a steady reminder that this moment—this gathering of laughter and light—was hard-earned and deeply cherished.

Somewhere between bites of her meal and a story O'Neal was animatedly telling, Izzy's gaze drifted again. She looked around the table, at the faces she loved, and felt the fragile beauty of their togetherness. The warmth of the restaurant, the sound of silverware clinking against plates, and the hum of nearby conversations wrapped around her like a soft blanket.

It was a stark contrast to where they'd been just weeks ago, in the depths of the woods, surrounded by fear and violence. She thought of the other women again, wondering if they'd found their own moments of light. A quiet prayer rose in her heart, a plea for their healing and peace.

She felt Gabe's hand slip into hers beneath the table, his thumb brushing gently against her knuckles. When she turned to him, he wasn't looking at her; he was listening to her father with rapt attention. But that small touch spoke volumes.

You're here.

You're safe.

You're loved.

"'For I know the plans I have for you,' declares the Lord, 'plans to prosper you and not to harm you, plans to give you hope and a future'" (Jeremiah 29:11).

IZZY

One Year Later

Sweat trickled down Izzy's temples, tracing her neck and disappearing beneath her shirt. Each breath came in sharp, controlled heaves as she darted forward, throwing a quick jab. Gabe countered effortlessly, blocking her strike with his forearm. She pivoted, aiming a calculated elbow at his side, but he ducked, slipping around her like water over rocks.

"Too slow," he teased, his lips quirking into that infuriating, smug grin she both loved and hated.

She ignored him, shifting her weight to her left leg and feinting a punch with her right. When he leaned to deflect, she struck low with a sweeping kick aimed at his shin. But he was faster—always faster. His arm hooked her waist in one fluid motion, lifting her off balance and sending her sprawling onto the mat with a solid thud.

The ceiling lights swirled in her vision as her lungs fought to catch up. Gabe crouched over her, his silhouette haloed by the gym's fluorescent glow. "Gotcha again," he said, his voice a blend of amusement and triumph.

"Yeah, yeah," she muttered, taking the hand he offered and letting him haul her up. Her eyes zeroed in on the gold band gleaming on his left hand as he flexed his fingers. Even drenched in sweat and wearing his usual gray tank and loose shorts, the sight of him stole her breath in an entirely different way.

"You know, for a ninja master, you're not very humble," she said, mock exasperation dripping from her words.

His brows lifted, his smirk deepening. "And for a journalist, you're not very sneaky."

She stuck her tongue out at him and darted forward, aiming a playful jab at his ribs. But before she could land the hit, his arms wrapped around her, tackling her gently to the mat.

"Say it," he demanded, his fingers digging into her sides, sending shockwaves of laughter through her.

"Never!" she gasped, squirming under his relentless tickling.

"Say I'm a ninja master!"

"You—" she squealed as he pinned her legs and went for her feet, her laughter morphing into near-hysterics. "Okay, okay! You're a ninja master!"

"Say it louder," he said, grinning wickedly.

"You're a ninja master!" she yelled through her giggles, tears streaming down her cheeks.

Satisfied, he relented, bracing his hands on the mat to look down at her. Their laughter faded into a comfortable quiet, the air between them thick with unspoken joy. He leaned closer, brushing a damp strand of hair from her face.

His voice dropped, rich and low, as he nuzzled her neck with the soft stubble of his face. "I love you, Izzy." Her insides tingled in response, both from his touch and his words.

Her heart thudded harder—not from exertion this time, but from the way he looked at her, like she was the only thing in the world worth seeing.

"One more match, and then we'll head home," Izzy's mind perked up at the word.

Home. The little house they'd found together was a wonderful find. On the outskirts of Charlotte, close to her father and Sophie. Green grass stretched out for an acre in a beautiful yard for Marshall to run wild in. The largest bay window she'd ever seen adorned the front room, and Gabe knew it had stolen her heart the moment they laid eyes on it. Still, she knew it was merely a house. *He* was her home now.

"Fine. But it better be quick. And none of those leg sweeps, *ninja master.*" She pointed her finger at him as she got to her feet, gesturing to his powerful legs. He raised his hands in mock defense, angling his head toward her in agreement, unable to stop the grin on his lips.

Izzy attacked without giving him the opportunity to think. Right then left, crouching like he'd taught her to find an opening for a body shot. Gabe deflected, matching her with ease. Grinning like a proud fool as she put into practice all he'd taught her. He insisted on these lessons ever since she'd agreed to be a liaison to the Special

Investigations Unit. Neither of them knew what the future held, but he knew he couldn't always be there to protect her. Having already proven herself capable, he'd said he wanted her to be *unstoppable*. And truthfully, Izzy relished the idea of being able to bring a man to his knees with her bare hands.

This time, she caught him off-guard, forcing him to defend against a rapid succession of strikes she threw his way. When she saw his focus on her blows, she went in for the final blow. Dodging left, he threw all of his weight into anticipating a block that struck nothing but air. Balance off-kilter, she struck him in the mid-section with a merciless uppercut. The move knocked the wind from him, and he doubled over, a laugh mixed with a groan escaping his lips.

"Cheap shot," he managed between breaths, his grin belying his words.

Izzy grinned foolishly as she tried to catch her breath, her heart rate fluttering impossibly high in her chest. Her head spun dizzily, her brain still racing after her body had stopped. Her satisfaction was short-lived as her stomach twisted sharply. Her mouth began to water, pins and needles dancing on her cheeks and jaw as nausea overcame her. Stumbling to the trash can, she heaved violently, emptying the contents of her stomach until there was nothing left.

"Whoa, hey," Gabe was beside her in seconds, one hand on her back and the other holding out her water bottle. His brow furrowed as he watched her carefully. "You okay? What was that?"

She shook her head, her thoughts racing. A calendar in her mind flipped backward, tallying days. Her hand fell instinctively to her abdomen as realization struck.

"Oh." The word came out as a whisper, as her jaw hung slack.

Gabe's eyes followed the motion, his expression shifting from confusion to something deeper—hope, disbelief, joy all rolled into one. He stepped closer, his voice hushed. "Yeah?"

Tears welled in her eyes as she nodded, her throat too tight to form words.

A slow grin spread across his face, and then he moved. Sweeping her into his arms, he lifted her off the ground, spinning her in a wide circle, whooping with joy. His laughter was pure and unrestrained, a sound that filled the gym like sunlight piercing a storm.

"You're serious?" he asked, his voice cracking with emotion as he set her down gently. Like she was something precious.

Izzy nodded again, a watery laugh escaping her lips. "We're having a baby, Gabe."

He cupped her face in his hands, his thumbs brushing away the tears that streaked her cheeks. "I can't believe it," he murmured, his voice thick with awe.

"Believe it, ninja master."

He laughed, kissing her soundly. "I love you," he whispered against her lips.

The drive home was quiet, the kind of silence that spoke volumes. Their little house appeared in the distance, the warm glow of its porch light welcoming them back. Marshall greeted them at the door, his tail wagging furiously as he circled their legs.

Izzy sank onto the couch, her hands resting on her belly as they waited anxiously for the confirmation they sought.

Two pink lines. She didn't need the directions this time to know what they meant. The future stretched out before her, uncertain but full of promise. She glanced at Gabe, his hands on his head in disbelief. His expression was one of both terror and joy. Marshall tried to nose between them as Gabe pulled her into a tight embrace that said everything.

At that moment, she knew. Everything—the pain, the trials, the triumphs—had led her here. And it was worth it.

She placed her hand over Gabe's as he sat beside her. Together, they looked toward tomorrow, their hearts full and ready for whatever came next.

GABE

The following June, at 7:23 a.m., our child came into the world. A piercing cry shattered the quiet of the delivery room, raw and vibrant, a sound that reverberated through me, rooting me to the spot. My knees almost buckled at the rush of emotions that hit me: awe, relief, gratitude, and something deeper—something primal.

"It's a girl," the doctor announced, her voice warm and steady despite the whirlwind of activity around us.

Hope Sophia Walsh.

The name had been a quiet agreement between us, unspoken until it was decided. Hope—for all we'd fought for, all we'd lost, and all we'd gained. Sophia—for the friend Izzy had nearly lost and had fought so fiercely to save. The friend who, through a flurry of circumstances and divine intervention, brought us together. And Walsh... that part still felt surreal, as if I were living in someone else's story.

"Do you want to cut the cord, Dad?" the nurse asked, her words pulling me back into the moment.

Dad.

The title felt foreign and enormous, but it settled into me as naturally as the air filling my lungs. I nodded, stepping forward with shaky hands to take the sterile scissors. As I cut the cord, severing the final physical tie between my daughter and the woman I loved, a sense of completeness washed over me.

"She's perfect," I whispered, my voice breaking as I turned to Izzy.

Her face was pale with exertion, her hair plastered to her damp forehead, but she was glowing. Literally glowing. The moment her eyes found mine, I knew I'd never love anyone the way I loved her. Not even close.

"Let me see her," Izzy said, her voice hoarse but steady.

The nurse carefully placed our daughter on the warm skin of Izzy's waiting chest, covering her in a soft pink blanket. She whispered, "you did good, mama" in Izzy's ear as I watched my wife cradle our child for the first time – her fingers trembling as they brushed the baby's downy hair.

"Hi, Hope," Izzy whispered, her lips curving into a teary smile. "Welcome to the world, sweet girl."

I leaned in, resting my forehead against Izzy's, the three of us cocooned in this moment of pure, unfiltered joy. Hope's cries softened, and she blinked up at us with wide, curious eyes.

"She's got your eyes," Izzy said, her voice thick with emotion.

"And your fire," I replied, my chest tightening as I traced the tiny curve of Hope's cheek with my finger. "She's everything."

The enormity of the moment settled over us like a warm blanket, grounding me in a way I hadn't felt in years. Every scar, every wound, every mistake—it all led here. And as I held my daughter for the first time, her tiny fingers curling instinctively around mine, I knew I'd do anything to protect her, to give her the life she deserved.

"I can't believe we made her," Izzy said softly, her gaze never leaving Hope's face.

I smiled, pressing a kiss to her temple. "You did all the hard work. I just showed up at the right time."

She laughed, a sound that made my heart lighter than it had been in years.

Hours later, as the morning sun filtered through the hospital room window, I watched my two girls sleeping. Izzy's head rested against the pillows, her hair a wild halo around her face. Hope lay nestled against her chest, her tiny body rising and falling in rhythm with her mother's breaths.

Marshall would be waiting for us at home, probably pacing the living room in anticipation. The thought made me smile, and I made a mental note to sneak him a treat for being so patient.

For now, though, I stayed rooted in that chair beside the bed, unable to look away from the two people who had become my entire world.

Hope Sophia Walsh.

Her name was a promise—a beacon for the future we'd fight for, no matter what.

And for the first time in a long time, I wasn't afraid.

I was ready.

ABOUT THE AUTHOR:

A. A. Stevenson is a debut author with a passion for storytelling rooted in her faith and life experiences. Residing in Ohio, she balances her roles as a dedicated Registered Nurse, wife, and mother to two energetic boys. Writ ing has always been a cherished outlet for Stevenson, but it was her husband's encouragement that inspired her to bring her creative dreams to fruition and publish her first novel. Stevenson's journey to authorship began with a series of recurring dreams, each building upon the last, sparking an idea that grew into a capti vating story. Drawing from her love of the outdoors and a deep appreciation for character development, she enjoys crafting narratives that explore re silience and hope amidst adversity. Her faith in Jesus Christ serves as the foundation for her work, and she aspires to leave readers with a sense of hope and encouragement, even in the face of suffering. While not writing, Stevenson can be found working as a registered nurse, spending time with her family, camping under starry skies, or enjoying music. Though she's read widely, she doesn't attribute her writing style to a singular influence, instead embracing a unique voice shaped by her life's tapestry. Stevenson is active on TikTok and Instagram, where she connects with readers and shares glimpses into her life and creative process. With her debut novel, she invites readers to join her on a journey of faith, resilience, and dis covery—and hopes her stories inspire others to seek the beauty and hope that can be found even in life's most challenging moments.

www.ingramcontent.com/pod-product-compliance
Lightning Source LLC
Chambersburg PA
CBHW070529310726
48976CB00002BA/581